MURDER
IN
HARMONY

By

Jewel Deane Love Suddath

Jewel Deane Love Suddath
2004

ISBN: 1-4140-4245-0 (e-book)
ISBN: 1-4140-4243-4 (Paperback)
ISBN: 1-4140-4244-2 (Dust Jacket)

Library of Congress Control Number: 2003098946

This book is printed on acid free paper.

Printed in the United States of America
Bloomington, IN

1stBooks – rev. 01/15/04

Acknowledgments

I thank Marilyn Fast, Sue Ellen Frye, and Nancy Register for encouraging me and for taking time away from their own writing to help me edit mine.

And

I thank my husband, George Suddath, for sharing Georgia stories, for helping me research details, for reading every single chapter as I wrote, and for laughing at all the right places.

And

I thank Rob and Lorraine Garden for their professional computer detective work that enabled me to publish this novel about amateur detectives.

And

I thank Michael and Chris Frye for making suggestions about early portions of the book during a beach trip we shared years ago.

And

I thank Doug Heilman for explaining rifles, bullets, and shooting to me.

And

I thank Elizabeth Frye for advising me on behavioral motivation and psychological terminology.

And

I thank my dear friend, Grace Readling, for finding Edgar's old pictures of the Bayless Memorial Presbyterian Church choir.

And

I thank all the storytellers and colorful characters I've known in Concord, Red Springs, Laurinburg, Rocky Mount, Cary, Apex, Athens, and Raleigh.

This book is dedicated

to the memory of my daddy and mama,

Dock and Margie Love,

from whom I learned storytelling and other forms of giving,

and

to my sister,

Sue Ellen Love Frye,

with whom I shared

a loving family, a small town, and so many adventures.

Contents

Chapter 1

The $64,000 Question

Lots of people think Buck Eudy's crazy. Even Mama and Daddy, who seldom say an unkind word about anybody, allow that he's just a little bit off. Crazy, I'll give you, but Buck's no murderer, I don't care what anybody says.

Linda Sue and I don't miss a trick in this neighborhood. If it happens on Gibson Street, us Sparks girls know about it. Today was Good Friday, so we were home from school. It was me that saw the long brown county cruiser roll past our house just before *The Guiding Light*. I stumped my big toe trying to get around the vacuum cleaner to the picture window before it was gone. As it turned out, I didn't

1

need to worry about that because it pulled into Buck Eudy's dirt driveway right next door.

Believe me, a deputy sheriff's car is not a common sight on our street. Most of Gibson Street lies inside the Harmony city limits, so we're used to seeing John Law cruise our part of the neighborhood in black and white city police cars. But the six houses past ours are outside the city limits, and the county doesn't bother to patrol its part. I can't remember ever seeing a county deputy get out of his car on this street. Not till yesterday, that is.

Linda Sue spotted me at the window and yelled from the kitchen. "Jonnie Sparks, you'd better get that rug vacuumed, or you're going to be sorry when Mama comes home. I just left you one room." My little sister is a thirteen-year-old version of Harriet on *The Ozzie and Harriet Show.* Me, I hate housework.

I like to knocked her down trying to get to the back door. "Come on. The Law just pulled in over at Buck's."

"You sure?"

"Saw the gold star on his car door."

I beat her to the breezeway and out the screen door. She caught up with me at the crepe myrtle bushes Daddy planted last year between our house and Buck's vacant field. We dropped to our knees in the grass.

"Be still and they won't see us." I took her arm above the elbow and didn't turn loose.

The deputy stood on Buck's front porch knocking on the rusty screen door. He was a short man, maybe 5' 8", but his gray Sky King hat and his two-tone gray uniform made him seem taller. The brown leaves Buck's big oak had held through the winter didn't keep out much of the spring sunshine. The deputy or anybody else who might've been interested could see the white peeling off Buck's house and know it was overdue for a paint job, long overdue.

Buck's big dog Willie barked a couple times from the dust under the front corner of the porch but didn't bother to come out from his favorite spot. He's so old he doesn't even scare the little kids who play rollie bat in Buck's field after school. Buck finally answered the deputy's knock, but we couldn't hear a word that was said. After a minute or two, the deputy disappeared through the door. We tried to guess what brought him to Buck's house.

"You reckon Buck's filed a report about the FBI men he claims have been watching him?" I said.

"Nope, he'd have used our phone to do that, and he hasn't been over here in months."

Linda Sue put the thumb and four fingers of each hand together and then put them up to her blue eyes, playing like she was looking at Buck's old house through binoculars. She showed her crooked front teeth and imitated the song they used to play on *The $64,000 Question* while the contestant and all us watching on TV tried to figure out the answer to the question: "Dun, dun, dun, dee, dee, dee, dee, dee, dee." Her head jerked up and down and her blonde ponytail bounced as each word came out.

I need to explain that Buck has been mighty funny of late. I guess it started when he lost his teaching and coaching job out at

3

Stanly High School last year. Even before that, he was a little peculiar. Mama called him stubborn. Daddy said he was mule headed.

"I'm tired of squatting here," Linda Sue grunted. There's only three years difference in our ages, but sometimes she seems closer to ten than to thirteen.

"Hush, here comes somebody out."

Buck came first, his head hung low, his eyes fixed on the porch floor. He was wearing old dungarees and looked like he had a week's growth of beard on his bony face. The deputy was right behind him. They both stopped when Buck fished his keys out of his pocket and bent down to lock his front door. The deputy said something to him and pointed at Buck's old truck sitting down at the end of the driveway. They walked to it and Buck locked its doors. People on Gibson Street don't lock their doors unless they aren't going to be back for awhile. The only time Daddy locks ours is when we go to Carolina Beach the week the mill shuts down for July Fourth.

"I can't believe this is happening," Linda Sue whispered when the deputy and his prisoner started toward the patrol car.

"Me neither," I answered. "What could Buck have done?"

The deputy opened the back door of his car and held it for Buck to get in. Buck balled up his fists and his backbone got stiff. He looked every inch of his six feet. For a minute, I was afraid he was going to do something awful Then he raised his chin and spit a dark stream of tobacco juice across the driveway into the dust. The deputy put his hand on Buck's shoulder and nodded at the open car door. Buck folded himself up and squeezed into the back seat.

And they were gone.

* * * *

Just minutes later, Linda Sue and I heard a car roll down our driveway. We scrambled back across the front yard and barely gave Mama and Daddy time to slam our Chevy's doors before we started on our story. I led the way but every time I stopped to breathe, Linda Sue jumped in. She got to tell the best part, how mad Buck looked when he spit across the driveway.

"What you think, Daddy?" I asked. "Reckon they took him to Morganton?" I've heard my parents talk about people being put away in Morganton because they lost their minds. At times when she feels frustrated at us girls for one thing or another, Mama will look up over the top rim of the glasses that almost always sit at the end of her nose and say, "I feel like the next thing that pulls down our driveway will be the wagon coming to take me to Morganton."

"Nah, Buck ain't crazy. He's just quare, that's all." Daddy ran the fingers of his right hand through his wavy black hair. "I reckon I'd know that after living beside him all these years." He and Mama built our house here when old Commodore Eudy and Miss Lillie were alive and Buck was the only one of their children left at home. When we were little, my sister and I adopted the Eudys as our grandparents since three of our real ones had died years earlier.

5

Mama grew up on Gibson Street. She's always counted Buck as a friend. She raised her face so that she could look at Daddy, who stands a foot taller than her. "John, you don't reckon it's anything to do with that tale we heard at the mill around lunch time?"

Linda Sue grabbed Mama's wrist. "What'd you hear, Mama?" she said.

Mama's eyes never left Daddy's face. "The mess about the preacher's wife out at the Deliverance Tabernacle," she finished.

"Mrs. Gilmore? What about her?" I blurted out. "That's Luke's church, Mama."

Linda Sue rolled her blue eyes. She tries to act like she doesn't care much for my boyfriend, but like as not, there's some jealousy at work there. Thirteen's too early for a steady boyfriend, but that doesn't keep her from eyeing mine every once in a while.

"I know where Luke goes to church, Jonnie. You need to calm down." Mama's brown eyes nailed me to the ground and then returned to Daddy. She's barely five feet tall, but when she speaks in that tone of voice, Linda Sue and I know to listen. Daddy too.

Daddy rubbed his chin with his callused fingers. "There just might be a connection," he said. "Buck's been doing janitor work over there the last little while." You remember their preacher calling us up and asking whether we thought he was reliable enough to fit the bill."

"Yes, and other questions too," Mama nodded. There were worry lines between her eyebrows. "I was the one answered the phone. I told him Buck would be good at the job. I sure hope there's no connection."

"Connection with what?" I asked. "What did you hear about Mrs. Gilmore?"

The preacher's wife is surely no friend of mine. I had a run-in with her last summer when I first started dating Luke Goodman, and I've tried to steer clear of her ever since. Still, it shocked me to hear mama mention her when we were talking about Buck's arrest. I figured she must've accused him of stealing something from the church.

"Well, we don't know how much truth there is to it." Mama's voice was too cautious. That's the way she is.

"It won't hurt to tell us what you heard," I said. "If you don't want us to spread it—"

"Shoot," Linda Sue interrupted. "Everybody else on the first shift of Harmony Mills Plant 6 is spreading it at this very minute."

Daddy pointed his finger at her. "Be still for a minute," he said and then turned back toward Mama. "Lois, they're going to hear it sooner or later anyhow."

"I know that, John," she said, but she shook her head slowly from side to side like she didn't *want* to know it.

"If Mrs. Gilmore has got Buck in trouble, it won't be the first time she's stuck her nose in somebody else's business," I said softly.

"Yeah, but this time she sent a sheriff's deputy to do her dirty work," Linda Sue said. "She probably caught Buck spitting tobacco juice into one of his little pork 'n beans cans, and it made her mad."

7

"Yeah, and then she preached him one of her sermons," I agreed.

We'd gone too far. Mama's always saying we have too much imagination for our own good. With one sentence she put an end to the story we were about to make up. "You girls have got no idea what you're talking about."

Daddy nodded. "Your mama's right," he said. "It seems like an awful thing has happened." He looked from us to Mama. The two of them were quiet for a minute, but I knew they'd decided we could hear the story.

"We don't know any details, and like I said, we don't even know if it's true," Mama began. "But last night or this morning one, they found Mrs. Gilmore's body stuffed in the trunk of her car in the parking lot beside the church."

For just a second or two, I couldn't get my breath. "Oh no, Mama," I finally managed to choke out. "That can't be right."

"Who found her?" Linda Sue asked.

"We don't rightly know, and we got no business spreading half truths." Mama's never been one to gossip.

"How long's the deputy been gone with Buck?" Daddy asked me.

Linda Sue beat me to an answer. "Pulled out that driveway about five minutes after three."

"I wish y'all could've been here when Buck came out the door," I said.

"He didn't cause any trouble, I hope," Mama said.

8

"I told you how he clenched his fists and spit before he got in the car," Linda Sue had to get in her two cents worth.

I knew Mama would just as soon pretend foul language, fist fights, and highway accidents don't exist in Harmony. I threw a frown at my sister and said, "Yeah, but that's not what I'm talking about. When Buck first came out of the house, his shoulders were all slumped over, and his head was hanging almost down to his chest. He looked like an old man."

Mama's face got sadder. "That's exactly the way his daddy, Commodore, looked when they brought him home from the hospital the night Miss Lilllie died," she said.

"I just can't think Buck had anything to do with the trouble at that church," Daddy said, more to himself than to us. "I know he's been a different man since he lost that teaching job, and I think living by hisself over there has give him too much time to study on it. That's the reason he's got so quare, maybe a little touched." He rested his chin in his right palm like he was trying to figure it all out. "But I can't see him hurting anybody. No sir."

Mama nodded her head to agree with him. She was probably thinking of the years she'd spent growing up out the street from Buck. She never had a bicycle of her own, so he used to give her rides on the back fender of his. When she was in the eighth grade, he tried to talk her out of quitting school to go to work in Harmony Mills where her daddy worked. He lost that one.

"If that story about Mrs. Gilmore's true," I said, "I can think of more than one person in her very own church that she's made mad

9

these past couple years. Any one of them would have more reason than Buck to want her dead."

"And there's plenty of drunks in this town and bums roaming the railroad tracks," Linda Sue added. "One of them could've done it to get money."

"But then why did the sheriff's department come out here and haul Buck off?" I said.

"We've no cause to go jumping to conclusions," Mama said.

"Shoot! Luke Goodman would know what happened at his own church," Linda Sue said. "Call him up and find out, Jonnie."

"He'd still be at work at the drug store. Won't be home before six." I didn't want to call Luke. He does all the calling in our romance, always has. And he seldom calls more than twice a week, three times at best.

"Wonder if he even went to the drug store this afternoon?" My little sister wouldn't let the subject drop.

"Of course, he did. It's his job," I said.

"Not so fast," she said. "Didn't you tell me the people at the Tabernacle think of each other as family and sometimes Mrs. Gilmore acts like a big mama hen?"

"Maybe so. What if I did?"

"Luke Goodman wouldn't be at work if the mama hen was found dead like we think she was. Why don't you call? It won't hurt anything," she prodded.

I covered my eyes with my palms and considered for a minute before answering. "I'd rather wait and let Luke call me. That is, if he has any reason to call me." It was a lie. I was dying to know if Buck was connected to what Mama and Daddy had heard, but I knew Luke wouldn't take to me calling him, not even if murder was involved.

"*The Telegram* ought to be in the driveway pretty soon," Daddy said. He and Mama respect Harmony's little newspaper almost as much as they do the Harmony Methodist Church, where we're all members. He cut his eyes over to Mama and asked, "Don't you think it's bound to be on the front page, Lois?"

About that time, Sonny Calloway came tearing down our driveway on his beat-up red Schwinn. He was raring to talk about the news his mama had brought home from the mill. "Jonnie, your goody-goody boyfriend called you about that old Gilmore woman gettin' killed and crammed in the trunk of her own Plymouth?" he asked. His brown eyes were open wide.

Mama and Daddy started on into the house to wash up and get ready for supper. The water oaks beside our driveway hadn't sprouted any leaves yet this spring and today's sun was bright. I pushed my long hair back from my face and wiped a line of sweat off my forehead. Too late, I remembered the vacuum cleaner lying on our dirty living room floor. It'd just have to wait. I had news too good to keep.

"No, he hasn't called, but you won't believe what we saw."

Sonny's eyebrows remind me of wire brushes. They shoot up on his forehead any time he thinks somebody's going to give him juicy news. The wire brushes moved a half inch as I went on talking.

"John Law in the form of the sheriff's deputy cruised past our house not thirty minutes ago and turned in at Buck Eudy's driveway."

"Yeah," Linda Sue chimed in, "and he didn't leave till he had Buck in his back seat in custody."

"You're a lie." Sonny tried to act cool, like he wasn't really interested.

"Ask Jonnie."

"It's the truth," I said nodding my head hard, "and Daddy says there just might be a connection between Buck and the murder. Those are his very words."

He let out a low whistle and slapped his hands together. Sonny lives around the curve from Buck's house and outside the city limits. He's a sophomore at the county high school where Buck used to work, but he didn't take algebra when Buck was teaching it there. He speaks or waves when he sees Buck on the porch, but he's never been one of the boys who're in and out of Buck's house on weekends. Of course, he's seen them there. Everybody in the neighborhood has. They're boys from the baseball teams Buck coached at Stanly High. Years after they pitch their last game or make their last run for the school, they keep coming over to Buck's. Mama says they're the only children he'll ever have.

"I know he's been working out at the Tabernacle, but why the hell would he kill that Gilmore woman?" Sonny asked.

"She was never easy to get along with," I said. "Always finding fault."

"Tell him about you being a painted woman," Linda Sue said. Sonny raised his eyebrows.

I gave a half laugh. "One night I wore hot coral lipstick and green eye shadow when I went out there to a young people's meeting with Luke. I tied a lime scarf around my pony tail and looked good enough to turn more than one head that night, if I do say so myself."

"Maybe one head too many," my sister added.

"Next thing I knew, Mrs. Gilmore had put me in a talk she gave to the Senior High Sundcay School class. She claimed the Bible warns against painted women and told the whole class they should be careful of the company they keep."

"Shit! How'd you find out?"

"Luke told me. He was sitting right there in the class. He said he was awfully embarrassed and wished I'd just wear natural lipstick in the future and no eye shadow at all."

Sonny grinned and the skin around his eyes crinkled up. "And you told him?"

"I said I didn't see anything wrong with Mrs. Gilmore being a Plain Jane if that was what she wanted."

Sonny laughed. "I've never bumped into the woman," he said. "She's not much of a looker, huh?"

"She was probably born plain and she must want to stay that way." I shrugged my shoulders. "I told Luke she must've got her painted women out of a Bible at their church because I never heard of them in the ones we use at Trinity Methodist."

"Hot damn!" He laughed and laughed and laughed. "So, you think she made Buck mad enough for him to kill her?"

"No, I don't. I just said she wasn't easy to get along with. Sometimes it seemed like she was the preacher, not Rev. Gilmore."

"Hmm, a woman preacher." He scratched his chin. "Harmony's never had one of them."

"I promise you, there's more than one strange person at that church. I've been in some of their meetings these past eight months, and I could tell you a tale or two."

"Tell him what you saw at the Tabernacle's day camp that afternoon you drove out there to pick up Luke," Linda Sue said.

I gave her the evil eye and was relieved when Mama stuck her head out the door.

"She won't be starting any more stories right now," Mama said. "I got supper on the table getting cold. Sonny, your mama will be calling you to yours, too, any minute now."

"All right," he answered, "but I'll be back after supper. *The Telegram* will be here by then."

He jumped on his bicycle and spun off up the driveway.

Mama turned and went back into the house ahead of us girls. I stared at my sister long and hard and said, "You better hope Sonny forgets what you said about me seeing something peculiar at the Tabernacle's day camp. You hear?"

"It's a free country," she snapped.

Chapter 2

Headlines

At supper, we tried to make sense of the news Mama and Daddy brought home from the mill and what Linda Sue and I saw next door. I was in the middle of my second hot dog when I heard *The Telegram* hit the gravel outside. That whump in the driveway ended supper for Linda Sue and me, but I knew better than to leave the table until we all finished. Daddy made him a third hot dog and didn't break any records getting it down.

Finally, he got up and started out the door to bring in the newspaper. I went with him so we were the first to see page one. The biggest and blackest headlines I've ever seen topped the page. MINISTER'S WIFE SLAIN.

"Here." Daddy handed me the paper. "You read it out loud when we get inside." My daddy can't read very good. He couldn't read at all until he married Mama. Grandpa Sparks was a sharecropper and needed him in the fields a lot of the time he should've been in school. Mama's daddy, Grandpa Beech, was a teacher in a one-room schoolhouse before he moved to town to work in a mill. When Mama married Daddy, Grandpa Beech taught Daddy to read and write. He reads the newspaper every day and picks up the *Reader's Digest* sometimes, but I've never heard him try to read out loud.

We went back into the kitchen, and all four gathered around the table again. I read from *The Telegram* in a solemn voice. I felt like it was one of those yellow telegrams I'd heard Mama say Grandma Beech got when Mama's brother was killed in the war.

> The body of Eunice Fay Gilmore, 51, was found dead in the trunk of her 1950 Plymouth in the parking lot beside the Deliverance Tabernacle of Faith on Highway 42-A. No suspect has been arrested at this time.

"Well, we know better," Linda Sue said.

> Authorities discovered the body at 10:15 PM Thursday after her husband, Earl T. Gilmore, pastor of the Tabernacle, reported she had not returned home from a pre-Easter cookout given for the church youth. Rev. Gilmore had attempted to telephone his wife and finally walked to the church to look for her. Upon

finding blood on the stairs leading to the church basement, he telephoned the sheriff's office.

Sheriff Shepherd reports that death was caused by several blows to the head from a large push broom and by a concussion the victim suffered when she collapsed backward and hit her head on the cement steps. Her body was then dragged across the basement and through the side door and placed in the trunk of the couple's car.

Billy Mack Barrier, a member of the Tabernacle's softball team, says he and Mrs. Gilmore were about to leave the church grounds around 9 PM when she told him she had forgotten to get a folder her husband needed from his office. She insisted the boy go on home and he did.

Young Barrier says Sheriff Shepherd plans to question other members of the softball team to help him get some leads.

"Softball sleuths," Linda Sue snorted.

The Gilmores moved to Harmony in 1949 and have been at the Tabernacle for nine years. They reside in the church parsonage one half mile west of the church. Mrs. Gilmore took an active role in leading the congregation from the very beginning. She was director of the church choir, which won five district denominational competitions under her supervision. She often sang solos during services at the church. Billy Barrier says the preacher and his wife were a team that was hard to beat.

"And Jonnie Sparks could testify that Mrs. Gilmore by herself was hard to bear."

"Linda Sue, that'll be enough," Mama pushed her glasses up on her nose. "You are not going to sit there and speak ill of the dead."

"But it's the truth, Mama, the honest truth." Linda Sue has a hard time holding her tongue sometimes. I think it runs in my family.

"I don't want to have to tell you again, Linda Sue. Why don't you and Jonnie clean up the supper dishes and take the table scraps over to Willie. See if you can find an old tin pan in the car shed to put them in. I know Buck didn't have time to feed him today."

The phone rang and I jumped for it.

"Jonnie, I guess you heard the bad news?" It was Luke. About time.

"I saw *The Telegram* but I still can't believe Mrs. Gilmore's dead. It's the worst thing that's happened to anybody I know since that hobo stabbed Uncle Raymond outside the liquor store."

"Yeah and it's worse than you think."

"Did Tubby Shepherd question you like he did Billy Mack?"

"He talked to most of us on the team. It's a good thing he did."

"Why?"

"We helped him make an arrest. That's why."

"Huh?" I didn't like the way this conversation was going.

"Well, you know it rained last night. We had moved the cookout inside to the fellowship hall in the basement. That meant the basement had to be cleaned up afterward. Me, Grady, and Billy Mack hung around after most of the others left. Sister Gilmore saw us and told us to make ourselves useful and gather up all the paper plates and stuff. So we did. About that time, up came Buck Eudy with a mop and a big old wooden push broom."

"Listen Luke, Linda Sue and I saw—"

"Hold on, Jonnie. There's more. Buck put the broom in Billy Mack's hands and told him to start sweeping the floor. He said the basement looked like all hell had broke loose in it. Right there in the church, he said that."

"So what happened?" As far as I'm concerned, there's not much love lost between me and Luke's buddies at the Tabernacle. They're smart alecks. I wouldn't give ten cents for all their brains put together.

"Sister Gilmore heard him and she let him know in no uncertain terms there's no place for such talk in the Lord's House. Then she took that broom away from Billy Mack and put it back in Buck's hands. She looked him right straight in the eye and said, 'Now, I suggest you do the job this church is paying you to do and let these boys finish the task I gave them.'"

I gritted my teeth. "And how did Buck take that?"

"First thing he did was to slam that push broom on the floor. Ker-blam. But to top it all, he spit tobacco juice on the floor too."

"She pushed him too far," I said.

"No, she didn't. She put him in his place. He was in the wrong."

"What happened next?" I asked my boyfriend who'd made himself into my neighbor's judge and jury.

"Buck stomped up the basement stairs two at a time and was gone."

"So y'all had to clean up the mess after all?" I asked.

"No, we intended to, but Sister Gilmore was upset."

"I bet so. She's not used to having anybody cross her."

I heard Luke let out his breath hard. "She said we were the guests at the cookout, not the cleanup crew," he finally said. "She told us to leave the janitor's work to the janitor. We tried to get her to let us sweep, but nothing would do but we go on home. So we did."

"Luke, y'all were the last ones to see her alive."

"Oh no, Buck Eudy was the last."

"I thought he got mad and stomped out."

"Don't you see?" Luke sounded like he was talking to his ten-year-old brother. "Buck Eudy never has been one to get along with people. He lost his job at my school because he thought he knew more than the principal."

"You haven't known him as long as I have. He pulled me through algebra when I was in ninth grade. I was on his front porch for help after school three days out of five."

"No matter. You told me yourself he's been acting crazy since he lost his teaching job. Growing toenails long as a hawk's. Talking about FBI men spying on his house."

"But I never said—"

"It was easy enough for Sheriff Shepherd to fit the pieces together after we told him what we knew." My boyfriend was proud of himself. "Directly after questioning the team, he phoned a deputy

20

and ordered him to get out to Buck's house and arrest him." I heard a smirk in his voice.

"That's enough," I said. "I don't need to hear another word. In fact, I'm hanging up right this minute." I slammed the receiver down.

Crazy, I'll give you, Luke Goodman. But Buck Eudy's no murderer. I don't care what you and Sheriff Tubby Shepherd say.

Chapter 3

The News Spreads

A *Closed* sign hangs on the door of my law office today. That's because it's Good Friday. That term has always seemed like a misnomer to me. Nobody in his right mind would argue that it was a good day for Jesus. Then there's the men who convicted and killed him. They don't make the human race in general or legal authorities in particular look like clubs anybody would want to belong to. I, myself, have practiced law in Harmony, North Carolina, for almost forty years. Like it or not, I guess I'll have to plead guilty to membership in both groups.

In our little town, lots of folks take Good Friday off. A few take Easter Monday too. I knew there wouldn't be a handful of people show up at my office today, so I decided not to show up myself. If anyone takes a sudden notion to have Clayton Wilkie draw up a will Friday, March 28, 1958, they're going to be disappointed.

The only drawback I could see to this arrangement was I might be spending the entire day with my good wife Maizie, who retired from a teaching position at Harmony High School ten months ago. Not that I don't like her company. Forty years of marriage and our knot is still secure, but her retirement has changed the way we spend our time together. Maizie loves to talk. For thirty-some years her American history classes satisfied a need I sometimes feel she now expects me to satisfy. She used to have a hundred fifty students to talk to. Isn't that what's called a captive audience? Now she has just me. Would it be rude to walk away from some of her lessons, or should I just give in and be the captive husband every weekend and every holiday? I've toyed with the idea of buying her a dog this Easter instead of giving her an orchid corsage like I usually do. Maybe a little cocker spaniel.

Every Friday at twelve noon, Maizie travels across town to have Boots Walls wash and set her hair. Her trips to the beauty shop give my ears a little rest and provide me an hour to work on my collection of political campaign badges. I don't know what my wife pays Boots, but whatever it is, it's not enough. Hairdressers ought to be paid by the hour to listen to people unload what's bothering them. That's the way it works with psychiatrists.

23

This Friday, however, it wasn't Maizie who did the talking. Still, she got her money's worth from the appointment. One of Boots's morning customers had come in with a story that would curl any woman's hair, and Boots did her part to see that her other customers got its details. Seems the wife of the preacher at Deliverance Tabernacle of Faith, a Pentecostal church on the outskirts of Harmony, was discovered dead in the trunk of the couple's car last night. Boots got to break a story in her beauty shop today that I doubt she'll ever top.

In Harmony people die normal deaths. Oh, from time to time, a drunk will die on the side of the railroad tracks from exposure. Occasionally, someone dies in a car wreck. Eight or ten years ago a woman named Byerly was murdered down near Black Bottom where a white woman has no business being in the first place. But by and large, people around here ride out of this world on the backs of pneumonia, heart attacks, strokes, or old age.

At one o'clock when she came home to me, my retired wife got her chance to break big news to her lawyer husband. I know she was glad I hadn't gone to the office today and she'd beat *The Harmony Telegram* by three hours. She talked nonstop while she made sandwiches and I poured tea for lunch. Before we ever got our food on the table, I'd learned what Maizie, Boots, and each of Boots's morning customers believed to have caused Mrs. Gilmore's death.

It is my experience that people like to claim some personal tie to a tragedy such as this. "How could she be gone?" someone might ask. "She helped me figure out the alto part in an anthem at choir practice last Wednesday night." That kind of thing. Maizie proved to be no exception. Over our pimento cheese sandwiches, she asked, "Clayton, what are we going to do about Sylvia?"

"What is her problem?" I answered without having any hint that my wife's concern for her twenty-two-year-old niece was tied to the murder we'd talked about for the past ten minutes.

"It isn't a problem yet but it could be," she said. Her expression was earnest. "You know she took on the job of playing the piano for that church's choir practice and Sunday morning service. I never thought it was the right thing to do, her and her family being Lutherans. And now this."

"Do you think Sylvia could afford to give up that job?" I said.

"At this point, I don't think she has much choice." Maizie stared at me like I was one of her students who'd answered *Robert E. Lee* when she'd asked the name of the Yankee general who burned Atlanta.

The Tabernacle folks are real proud of their choir. I know that from my friend, Jaybird Blanton, who hasn't missed a Sunday there in twenty years. He's got an attendance badge with a bar hanging on it for each of the years. When I go into Mabel's Red Pig to get my lunch on Tuesdays, Jaybird's usually sitting at the counter eating a barbeque sandwich. He seldom misses telling me about the music his church's choir produced the previous Sunday. How "Yield Not to Temptation" brought three young people to the altar rail at the end of a sermon. How the altos added harmony to "Day Is Dying in the West" during a revival service. How some woman with the unlikely name of Selma

Clinkscale sang like an angel during a denominational choir competition. When church people feel that strongly about their music, they're going to be mighty distressed to lose both their choir mistress and their pianist in one week. I was in no hurry to support Maizie's qualms.

"How much do you think Sylvia earns giving piano lessons to the pupils she's managed to drum up since she stopped looking for a real job?" I asked. "Majoring in music at Lenoir Rhyne College might be a decision she now regrets. I know her parents regret it."

"That's beside the point, Clayton. Last night a fifty-year-old woman was murdered at that church. Who's to say a pretty girl fresh out of college is safe traveling out there alone for Wednesday night choir practice?" Maizie got up and began taking our dishes off the table.

I carried my ice tea glass to the sink and then put my hand on my wife's back. "Tell you what," I said. "Easter or not, Deliverance Tabernacle won't be having any service this Sunday. They might meet with some other little church in the area, but they surely won't be needing Sylvia to play the piano."

"Guess not," she agreed.

"Well, you can invite her to attend church with us. Ask her to go to Morrison's for lunch afterwards too."

My wife's face lit up in a smile. "Good idea, Clay."

I returned her smile. "Sylvia might need to air her feelings about what's happened at that church. She can't drive all the way to the retirement village in Florida to talk to her mama and daddy. Call her right now."

So I was able to calm down my wife, who was more concerned about her perfectly healthy niece than she was about the murdered woman. Myself, I could hardly wait until *The Telegram* arrived at four.

Chapter 4

The Hum Dinger

We had barely finished drying the dishes when Sonny Calloway shot down our driveway again. He let his Schwinn fall beside the car shed without bothering to put the kickstand down and knocked on the breezeway screen. Mama saw him out the window and caught me before I could get to the door. "Jonnie, that vacuum's in the middle of the living room floor exactly where you left it. I asked you to help me clean up for Easter, but Linda Sue says you haven't done a lick of work all day."

She turned to put a coffee cup on the cabinet shelf, and I crossed my eyes at my sister. "But Mama, you know good and well I'm going to do my part."

"I don't want you leaving this house until the vacuuming's done. We don't ask much of you girls."

I kicked the toe of my loafer against the stove drawer, but I knew she was right. I bit my tongue to keep from backtalking her and started for the living room.

As she walked across the kitchen to the breezeway, Linda Sue gave me a phony smile. "I'm going on out and talk to Sonny," she said.

"Okay, but keep your trap shut about the day camp." I was in the living room out of Mama's sight, so I raised my fist and shook it in my sister's direction.

After I finally finished the living room rug and put up the hateful Electrolux, I found Sonny and Linda Sue on the breezeway steps. He was picking gravel out of Daddy's driveway and throwing it toward the big pear tree beside the car shed. If Daddy saw what he was doing, he'd come out and let him have it with both barrels.

"Wonder if John would let you take the Chevy up to the Hum Dinger? Wouldn't a cold drink hit the spot?" he said. Sonny is close to a year younger than me, and he doesn't have his drivers' license. Turning sixteen probably won't make much difference to him. His mama doesn't own a car.

"It can't hurt to ask," I said. "Stay right here. I'll find out."

A few minutes and I was back with the keys. I'd stopped long enough to dab on some lipstick and run a brush through my hair. It's black and naturally wavy like my daddy's and looks real pretty when I let it hang down on my shoulders. I'm not Liz Taylor but I *am* pretty. That's a fact.

Sonny and I started for Daddy's blue and white Chevy. Linda Sue brought up the rear.

"When's your daddy going to trade this thing?" Don't even have a radio. What year is it anyway, '51?"

"It's a '52 and it sure beats walking, Sonny Calloway," Linda Sue snapped. "Even if your mama had a car, she'd know better than to let you drive it."

That took the wind out of his sails. He sprawled in the back seat not speaking until I pulled into a stall at the Hum Dinger. We honked for Clem Ketner to come take our orders.

"What can I do for y'all?" Clem whined, sounding like he ought to be singing soprano in the choir out at the colored church on Lincoln Road.

"You need to give us a minute, Clementine. We just got here." Sonny's like every other white boy in Harmony. They rag Clem to no end. To my way of thinking, they do it to make themselves look big.

"Well, I wish y'alls would hurry up. I swan I do."

"Tell you what, Darlin' Clem. You bring us three Pepsis." Sonny was talking louder than he needed to.

"Hold it a minute," Linda Sue said. "I want a cherry Coke."

"Two Pepsis and one cherry on the way. I be right back." Clem sashayed off.

"Watch his behind," Sonny laughed. "It looks like two hogs fighting in a croker sack."

"You sound like our Daddy's Uncle Lefty before T.B. took him," I answered, not smiling.

"Yeah," Linda Sue agreed. "He never knew when to shut up."

"Sorry," Sonny said. "You talk, Jonnie. What did you start to say about the Tabernacle's day camp before you had to go to supper?"

Linda Sue interrupted before I could answer. "Forget it. Luke called her during supper to brag about how him and his softball buddies helped Tubby Shepherd solve Harmony's crime of the century. Ask her about that."

At first I said I'd rather not talk about the murder, but I ended up spilling the story after all. It was a good way to take Sonny's mind off the day camp. I knew he would get around to asking his same question again if I gave him enough time. That's one story I have no intention of telling him or anybody else. I hate to think what Luke might do if I did.

Just as I finished telling about hanging up on Luke, Clem appeared again. I thought of a way around my problem. "You can take the tray back now," I said as I reached to get the drinks. "We need to leave, Clem."

"Jonnie, we just got here," Linda Sue said.

"It's Friday night," Sonny agreed. "You ain't got no homework tonight. And didn't you tell me Luke always goes out with that bunch of boys over at his church on Fridays?"

"Yep. Friday after Friday."

"Wonder what they find to do every Friday," he said. "Speak in unknown tongues?"

Linda Sue cackled. She loves to make fun of Luke's friends. "Maybe the Tabernacle boys tore down all those tombstones out at Harmony Memorial Park awhile back," she said. "It's less than a mile from their church."

I blew my breath out like I was thinking of starting up the Chevy.

"I'm serious," Sonny said. "Don't you ever get jealous of them boys?"

I turned around catty-cornered in the seat so I could see his face. His brown eyes weren't laughing. "Yes, I do," I said.

"Don't any of the rest of them have girlfriends?"

"Billy Mack Barrier dates girls from the county schools, but nobody steady. To hear J.B. Blanton talk, you'd think he's had every cheerleader in this county at the Starlite Drive-In at one time or another. He calls it *the passion pit.* Grady and Parks Peacock never go anywhere with girls. I don't know why not. They look like they could be James Dean's kid brothers."

"You think they're as handsome as Luke?" Linda Sue asked. She'd turned around in her seat too.

"They come close."

32

"I'd call them pretty, not handsome," Sonny offered.

I looked at him for a minute almost smiling. His brown eyes and dark skin are the closest things to handsome that Sonny Calloway has going for him. He's always been big for his age. Big and chunky. The crewcut he wears doesn't do much for him either. His dark brown hair has too many cowlicks to stand up right. He walks out of the barbershop looking like somebody came after his head with a buzzsaw.

"*Pretty*'s for girls, Dumbhead," Linda Sue said.

"Yeah, I know," he answered. He waited for his words to sink in and then looked back at me. "Where y'all go on your Saturday dates, over to Charlotte?"

"No, we stay around here."

He raised his wiry eyebrows like he couldn't believe what I'd said. "What's to do here?" he asked. "Go downtown and watch the clock on the square tick off the minutes? If I had me some wheels, I'd hit Charlotte every weekend."

"You might change your tune when you turn sixteen and have to buy gas to fill your tank," I said.

Truth told, I've wondered why Luke has never mentioned going to Charlotte for a date, except for one time when the Carter Family Singers were to be at his friend Cecilia Shoe's church on Sunday night. I've seen that girl blink her eyes at Luke when she visited the Tabernacle here in Harmony. I turned down Luke's invite because it seemed stupid to put my boyfriend on Cecilia's stompin' ground during my date."

33

"You could be right," he answered, "but someday I'm taking me a girl to the Open Hearth on Wilshire Boulevard," he said. "Gonna get us a pizza."

"You ever been there?" I asked.

"No, but I heard about it. And I don't mean just any girl either. She'll be my girlfriend."

I studied my friend's face and wondered who the girl would be.

"Luke says when Rev. Gilmore talks to their youth group, he emphasizes friends, not girlfriends or boyfriends," I said.

"The man's an adult and a preacher. What you think he's gonna say?"

"And then there's Mrs. Gilmore." I said. "I don't mean to speak ill of the dead, but she did everything in her power to keep the Tabernacle's youth group from noticing there are people of the opposite sex living in this town."

Sonny laughed so I went on. "*Don't* wear makeup. *Don't* wear tight sweaters. *Don't* wear shorts. I wonder if she ever made a *Do* list."

"Some nerve," Linda Sue said. "She and the Reverend never had any children."

"Probably never got past kissing," I answered.

"*If* they got that far," Sonny added. "I bet they had a time getting Red Byerly to forget kissing. Is he one of your boyfriend's Friday Night God Squad now?"

"No, I guess he's too old. What is he, twenty?"

34

"Cain't be that old. Eighteen maybe. I remember when he quit school."

"Eighteen or twenty then. I don't know but it doesn't matter. He hasn't been off the bottle long enough for Luke's friends to take him with them on Friday nights."

"Good Christian boys," Linda Sue mumbled.

Red Byerly is what my mama calls a sad case and my daddy calls a no-count. Mama would be quick to tell you the poor thing's mama had her first and only baby when she was too young to know how to take care of it. Daddy would let you know Red's mama used to whore around near Black Bottom. One Sunday morning she was found dead in the woods down there. I don't actually remember her, but I know her name was Rose.

For as long as I can remember, Red's daddy hasn't had a steady job. When Archie Byerly does find work helping some house painter or jackleg mechanic, he drinks up his paycheck. He and Red live hand to mouth most of the time, or at least they did until Eunice Faye Gilmore brought Red into the fold over at the Tabernacle.

Archie rents a house way out of town just off Highway 42 on Gurley Road. It looks for all the world like an old cardboard box plopped down in a dirt field. Funny how a housepainter can't get around to painting his own house. It's not the only one either. You can spot any number just like it in that area. Daddy says when he first moved to Harmony in 1924, tenant farmers lived in them. That was over thirty years ago. I say they're sorry excuses for houses today.

The Deliverance Tabernacle of Faith sits right in the middle of those old eyesores.

"I'd give anything to have been on a back pew at the Tabernacle that night when Red busted in drunk," Sonny said. "Give me the story one more time, Jonnie."

"You're trying to keep me from starting home," I said. Actually, I wanted to stay at the Hum Dinger myself now that Sonny had turned loose of the day camp story.

"No, I just know you got it from Luke Goodman, an honest-to-God eyewitness." He laughed. "Come on. You ain't got nothin' else to do anyhow."

I couldn't argue that. Mama and Daddy were sitting in the den right now watching Jackie Gleason on T. V. I can take a little of him, but some of his stuff makes me want to barf. That loud-mouthed Ralph Kramden reminds me so much of my cousin Bennie. He failed the tenth grade, but he does make touchdowns for the Harmony High football team. Any time the Sparks family gets together, you'd think somebody had given him a mike and said "Speak, Great One." I hate a know-it-all.

"Go ahead, Jonnie," my sister said.

"Okay I'll tell it. One Wednesday night about six months ago, Rev. Gilmore was conducting Prayer Meeting at the Tabernacle. Of course, the whole Goodman family was there. The church members who had some problem burdening their hearts gathered around the wooden prayer rail near the pulpit. Rev. Gilmore raised his voice in a prayer that moved several women to tears. One big mill worker standing by the prayer rail began to speak in an unknown tongue. 'Elihu, elihu, enofini, now.'"

"Come on, Jonnie, you made them words up," Sonny said.

"You want to hear this story or not?" I asked.

"Sorry. I'm listening."

"I admit I wasn't at the Prayer Meeting, but as close as I can remember, those were the words Luke said came out of the man's mouth.

"Then with no warning, another voice interrupted. 'Where is the harlot hiding?' Luke said it sounded a little like a line from scripture. Every eye popped open. There stood Red a few feet inside the church door. You know he's six feet tall, and that night his orange beard had a couple weeks' growth."

Sonny snickered.

"The Tabernacle people might've thought he was John the Baptist if he hadn't had a Four Roses bottle in one hand and a bright pink neck scarf in the other."

Sonny snickered again.

"'I said, where you hiding my mama?' he shouted. You can imagine the shock on the people's faces. Red's mama's been dead for years."

"'Rose Byerly. Which one of you's got her this time?' Then he waved the scarf back and forth and stumbled to the front where he collapsed across the prayer rail, just missing Miss Alma Terry."

"I thought her name was Irma," Linda Sue chimed in.

"You know who I mean. That tottering old prune who won't let the doctor take the cataracts off her eyes. Luke said she screamed something at Red before he hit the rail, but nobody could understand what she said."

"Probably in an unknown tongue," Sonny said.

"Well, it wasn't a minute before Mrs. Gilmore was up out of her choir seat and beside Red at the prayer rail. She stretched her arms out over him, and the sleeves of her white robe spread like fans. She reminded Luke of some sort of guardian angel."

"So that was the beginning of her campaign to save Red Byerly?" Sonny said.

"Yeah, she put him a cot in the church basement. Archie Byerly raised Cain about the Gilmores trying to take his boy. He claimed to have spent all his money bringing up Red and finally got him to an age where he could go out and work to help his daddy."

"Humph," Linda Sue grunted. "Nobody in Harmony would give Archie Byerly an award on Father's Day."

"Right," Sonny said. "Far as raising's concerned, his mama wouldn't got no prizes either. Red raised himself."

"That's for sure," I agreed.

"Least when my daddy left ten years ago," Sonny went on, "me and Jane still had Mama. When Rose Byerly was murdered, all Red had left was Archie. That's worse than nothing."

Linda Sue and I didn't speak again for the longest time. Sonny had never, and I mean never, mentioned his daddy to us before. Now, it was like he had pulled a bumblebee out of his pocket and put it on my arm. I was afraid to move or say anything. I might get stung.

"Wait a minute." I was glad he broke the quiet. "If Red's been sleeping in the basement of the Tabernacle, he might know something about the murder."

"You've hit on something," I said. "The building where they hold preaching services has a basement. If you open the door to the left of where the choir stands, you can see the stairs. The basement is really a fellowship hall. They hold their church dinners down there."

Linda Sue leaned forward in her seat. "Shoot fire, Jonnie. That's where Mrs. Gilmore was murdered."

"You reckon anybody told the sheriff about Red?" Sonny asked.

I thought for a minute. "Well, Luke never mentioned it and *The Telegram* didn't either."

"Maybe Luke and his team aren't as slick as they think they are," Linda Sue said.

"Somebody ought to call the sheriff and ask if he knows," Sonny said, looking dead straight at me.

"Or you could call Luke and ask him about it," Linda Sue added.

"No, I don't want to talk to him again today." I sucked the straw of my Pepsi till I hit bottom. "He's not home anyway. Remember?"

"Oh yeah. Out with the boys," Sonny said.

I knew he was trying to get a rise out of me so I ignored him. "He and I are going to the movies tomorrow night," I said. "That's soon enough to ask him."

"But Jonnie, Buck's sitting in the county jail," Linda Sue whined, her face all drawn up in a frown.

I knew what she was getting at and nodded. "It's ten o'clock. Let's go home and tell Mama and Daddy. We'll see what they say."

I cranked the car and we headed for Gibson Street.

Chapter 5

April Love

Pat Boone was singing "April Love," and he was singing right to me. Two feet wide on the drive-in screen, his blue eyes smiled through the Ford's windshield straight into mine.

". . . so if she's the one, don't let her run away."

"I love this song, don't you?" I sighed and touched Luke's hand but pretended it was an accident.

He moved it to smooth his blonde hair back behind his right ear before answering. "Did you know Pat Boone helps in the big Deliverance Tabernacle in Los Angeles? Sister Gilmore said he speaks at youth rallies out there."

I looked straight into eyes every bit as pretty as Pat's. "Yeah, you told me. Listen to the words. I wonder who wrote them, a man or a woman."

"A man, most likely."

Luke must have been absent the day his English teacher talked about Emily Dickinson.

"They sound like a real poem," I said. "I like the way the word *April* sounds? It reminds me of the way a robin chirps in April."

"Want a Co-cola? We could split one," he offered.

"No, not right now," I answered. But with my eyes I said, ". . . so if she's the one, don't let her run away."

"Well, I think I'll go get me one."

Then it was just Pat and me.

Early this morning Luke called to say he knew I was real upset about Sister Gilmore being killed; otherwise, I wouldn't have hung up on him last night. Sure, I was upset about her, but I was much more upset about Buck. He lives right beside me. When he was away from home in the Service, I adopted Miss Lillie and Commodore Eudy as my grandparents. After he came home and began teaching math out at Stanly High School, he helped pull me through my first run-in with algebra. It was just too much for me to take when Luke convicted Buck of murder last night. It still makes me mad to think about it.

When I hung up on Luke, I knew I might've been getting myself into a fix. We'd already planned to see *April Love* tonight, but I wasn't sure he'd follow through until I saw his black Ford roll down our driveway just before dark. I was so relieved I'd have cried if I hadn't been afraid it would mess up my makeup.

As we drove down Gibson Street, neither of us said a word about the murder. I didn't even tell him about Daddy calling Sheriff Shepherd this morning to let him know about Red sleeping in the Tabernacle's basement. Since *The Telegram* doesn't come out on Saturdays, I hadn't heard any official details about Buck's arrest except for what I read Friday. Of course, all sorts of stories ran through town today. Daddy said it beat any news in Harmony since the Japanese bombed Pearl Harbor.

I worked at Purifoy's Dry Cleaners today, like I do every Saturday. I always make six dollars, which Mr. Raymond Purifoy takes out of a big fat roll of bills he keeps in his pants pocket. It's money he went around in his panel truck and collected all afternoon from people who had clothes cleaned on credit during the month and never got around to coming in and settling up with him. The six dollar bills he gives me are usually dirty and wrinkly, but they're better than a check because Mr. Raymond never takes out any taxes or social security. That's okay by me. It means I have more to spend on tickets to Baker's Lake or the Putt-Putt after I put aside a couple dollars in my college savings.

People picking up their dry cleaning today talked to me about the help Luke, Grady, and Billy Mack gave the sheriff. To hear some of them, you'd think those three boys had solved the case. When my American history teacher came in to get her spring jacket, she asked me how it felt to be the girlfriend of a hero. I told her that last year my civics class learned a person is innocent until proven guilty. She laughed a short laugh and raised her black eyebrows like she couldn't quite believe I'd said that. Then she said, "Why Jonnie, Mr. Rimer would be proud of you."

"Thank you, Ma'am," I answered. By the time I left work, I'd had enough of people's talk about the part the Tabernacle boys played in my neighbor's arrest.

Luke took his time coming back from the concession stand. I put on the top sweater of the blue set my parents gave me for my last birthday and hugged myself tightly. My boyfriend and I have been dating for eight months now, ever since we met in August when our church softball teams were playing each other one Friday night. He doesn't go to Harmony High School, where I'm a junior. If he did, some other girl over there would have snagged him before I did. Somebody more popular than me. His house is ten miles outside the city limits, so he goes to Stanly High. He could have any girl there as his girlfriend because he's so good looking and he plays on their basketball team. I'm a lucky girl.

I was glad when Luke opened the car door and slid back under the wheel. He was careful not to spill any of the small fountain drink he'd bought. "Sure you don't want to split this?" he asked. He knows as well as I do that I like Pepsi, not Coke, but he seldom gives me a choice. Usually, he buys one drink and we split it. He has a little plan made out for the checks he gets from Diamond's Drug Store, and the first money to come out goes to the Deliverance Tabernacle. God gets a tenth but I don't get my own Pepsi at the drive-in.

"No, you drink it, but I do wish I had something heavier than this sweater set. My arms are cold. The weatherman said it would drop to thirty five tonight. Aren't you cold?"

"Not really. But I got the sweater you gave me for Christmas with me. Never can tell about March nights. Here, I'll get it for you." He found it in the back seat and draped it over my shoulders. Some people don't know a hint when it hits them in the face.

"Who'd you see up there?" I asked.

"JB was getting a drink. He's with that little blonde cheerleader from Landis."

"Y'all talk about the murder?"

"You know we did."

"Did the sheriff talk to him too?"

"No reason to. He wasn't at the cookout Thursday night."

"Huh?" As far as I can tell, JB Blanton dearly loves sexy girls, softball, and food—in that order. Since all three were plentiful at the cookout, I wondered why he'd missed it.

Luke took a deep breath and then let it out through his mouth like he was tired of my questions. "JB and Sister Gilmore had a falling out a couple months ago," he said. "He's been coming to church with his mama and daddy on Sunday mornings since then, but that's about all."

I knew I wasn't the only person she'd rubbed the wrong way. Not that I want to be put in the same boat with JB. He uses girls and then tosses them out the window like snotty Kleenexes. Me, I wouldn't give a dime for a dozen of him.

45

"What was the trouble about?" I asked. Luke kept chomping on a piece of ice from the bottom of his Coke cup.

"First off," he finally said, "she'd been giving him these little talks about bringing so many different girls to church parties and about missing young people's meetings on Sunday nights. Stuff like that."

"Uh hmm," I answered, trying not to show how interested I was.

"Then she went to JB's daddy. I don't know what she said to him, but it led to JB having to cut down his dates to just one a weekend."

Which is exactly how often we go out, I thought.

Like he'd read my mind, Luke said, "I don't see what JB got so mad about. Sister Gilmore was just interested in his well being."

"How mad did he get?" I asked.

He turned and fixed his eyes on mine. "Jonnie, you can't say a word about this to anybody. Okay?"

"Okay," I promised.

"One Saturday night in February, somebody took red paint and drew nasty pictures of Sister Gilmore on the back side of the church. It was on the outside wall of the choir loft where she directed our choir during preaching services. Sunday morning when Brother Gilmore went to open up the church, he found them. He called home and told Sister Gilmore what had happened. He advised her to stay home and said he'd get Selma Clinkscale to lead the choir during the morning service."

"That would've been right down Selma's alley," I said. "She loves to sing."

"Well, it didn't happen. Sister Gilmore refused to stay home. Not only that, she also got up during the service that morning and gave a talk on how people should try to understand the pictures were products of a sick, sick mind. She told us to remember the Bible teaches that vengeance belongs to the Lord."

I wondered why this news had never made it to *The Telegram.* "Did anybody report the pictures to the sheriff?" I said.

"No. I think Sister Gilmore wanted us to just go on about our business. Forgive and forget."

"If somebody drew nasty pictures of me on a church wall, I'd want people to forget it too."

Luke gave me a look that told me I'd said the wrong thing. "I'm not through," he said. "Let me finish. When she talked about vengeance belonging to the Lord, JB was sitting in the auditorium between his parents, and I was sitting right behind them. I don't know about his face but the back of his neck got red." Luke's mouth turned down at the corners, and he moved his head back and forth like he still had a hard time believing what his buddy had done.

"Have you said anything to him about it?" I asked.

"No, some of us boys talked about it after preaching was over, but JB and his parents went straight to the parking lot and left."

"Sounds suspicious to me."

"It's not like I was sure of anything, but a few days after that, I was kidding him about his daddy not letting him date but just once a week. He told me I'd better watch my mouth or somebody might paint the back of my house like they painted the back of the choir loft."

"That's a threat if I ever heard one. What did you say back?"

"JB has a temper. I knew to shut up. I haven't mentioned it since."

I couldn't believe my boyfriend had been sitting on this story. Maybe JB did the artwork or maybe he didn't. No matter, the sheriff ought to be told. "Luke," I said, "Mrs. Gilmore was killed Thursday night. The sheriff questioned you after the murder. Why didn't you tell him about the ugly pictures then?"

He shook his head. "It wasn't my place," he said. "Anyway, I know Elder Humpy Barrier or the preacher himself did that."

"But neither of them had any reason to connect JB to the drawings like you did." I said.

"JB never said he painted the wall. He wasn't the only person at the church who griped about Sister Gilmore." He thought for a minute and then added, "Come to think of it, Buck could have done it. Talk about a sick mind."

"You're sick yourself if you think you should keep quiet about what you know," I said.

Luke moved his hands close together and began popping his knuckles. First those on the left hand, then those on the right. "I've been praying for JB," he said.

What kind of answer could I give to that? I felt like hitting him up the side of his handsome face, but I knew it wouldn't change his

48

mind. I sat a long time, wondering how I could get Buck Eudy out of jail without losing my boyfriend.

Finally I said, "The murder is all I heard at work today. I spent more time answering questions about Buck Eudy's comings and goings than I did helping people with their dry cleaning."

"It was the same way at the drug store," he said.

"Most people were really down on him. It made me sad. Lots of them didn't know how Buck was working at two jobs since he stopped teaching. But the ones who'd brought their old clocks and watches to him to repair this past year agreed that he was handy at that. Some mentioned the FBI stories he'd tried to tell them. All of them talked about his beard and his dirty clothes."

"He was a sight, all right," Luke said. "A woman who came in to have a prescription filled today said she'd seen him barefoot on his porch with those inch-long nails curling under his toes. She said there used to be a colored preacher in Charlotte who had fingernails like Buck's toenails."

"Back when he taught math, he left for school every morning in a shirt and tie. I wonder what he was trying to prove these last months."

"The woman said the man in Charlotte painted red, white, and blue stripes on every fingernail. They called him Daddy Great or something like that."

"It's *Grace*," I said. "My Grandpa Sparks lives over in Charlotte," I said. "I've heard him talk about Daddy Grace. He thinks the man's doing it to draw attention to himself. I don't think that's Buck's reason."

Luke's face got real serious. "I had to go back to the sheriff's office again this afternoon," he said. "He asked me if Red Byerly had been at the cookout Thursday night. I told him Sister Gilmore always included Red when the church served food, and she did this time too. Red just ate a couple hot dogs and left early, by 7:30. I didn't see him after that. According to the sheriff, nobody's seen him since."

"Suspicious, very suspicious," I said.

"Maybe," he answered, "but maybe not."

"What you mean?"

"Red's known to drink. No telling when he might go off like this. I don't know why the sheriff kept asking questions about him. Good as Sister Gilmore was to Red, he'd never bother her. But Buck Eudy's another story. He resented her giving him orders."

Pat and Shirley's voices came through the speaker hanging on Luke's window. They sounded like they'd been singing together all their lives. I listened to their duet and thought about dropping my disagreement with Luke. But it was just for a minute.

"I wish you'd had Buck for algebra out at Stanly," I said. "Then you'd know him better. My mama grew up with him on Gibson Street in the 1920's. He was a little younger than her, a few years. She says he was always full of himself, looking for fun, spitting out a cuss word here and there, riding his bicycle all over Harmony. He was more daring than most people up there on the hill."

"Too bad his mama and daddy didn't know where he was headed. Mine would've."

"You're wrong, Luke. Mama's stories about him remind me of Sonny Calloway, always looking for excitement but not a mean bone in his body. Don't forget Buck grew up and went away to college."

"Yeah but—"

"If you knew him a little better, you might not be so quick to say he murdered Mrs. Gilmore and put her body in the trunk of her car. Buck couldn't do that."

Luke banged the steering wheel once with his fist. "Knowing him has nothing to do with it," he said. "Thursday night after the cookout Grady, Billy Mack, and me saw what we saw. Seeing is believing. That's what counts."

Luke stared at the screen like he cared what was going on in the movie. He was breathing hard, though. Pat and Shirley weren't doing anything to cause that.

"Tomorrow's *Telegram* will let everybody in Harmony know it was Buck's push broom that killed Sister Gilmore," he said.

Damn you, Luke Goodman, I thought. Then I swallowed hard to keep from saying it out loud. "There's got to be more to it than what you saw Thursday night." I said. "Sometimes you have to think past the things you can see. That's what Mr. White said in English class one day when he was teaching us about poetry."

"What has poetry got to do with Sister Gilmore being killed?"

I turned my face to the right and blew my breath on the car window. "Can you see who's in that car next to us?" I asked.

51

"No, their windows are fogged up, and now one of mine is too."

"Do you believe there's a couple in that car, even though you can't see them?"

"Yeah, yeah. I see what you're doing, but it's not the same."

"Just wait a minute," I said. "When you look at Buck, you see his brown button eyes and his crooked nose. You see a man in dirty dungarees with a wad of tobacco in his jaw. You see a janitor who didn't shave before he set out to clean your church's basement."

"Jonnie, it don't take some kind of x-ray vision to see things like that. It's plain something's wrong with Buck."

"But sometimes you have to think past the things you can see. Buck and Mr. White are the only people from Gibson Street to ever go away to college. I think it was something close to making history, them becoming teachers instead of going to work in Harmony Mills. Maybe you can't see what that means to the rest of us up on Mill Hill." I raised my arm and wiped the fog off the car window.

"Buck Eudy and Frank White are as different as night and day," Luke said. "Remember, Buck was fired from his teaching job."

"You don' know that," I snapped.

"Fired, suspended, let go—it's all the same. He lost his job."

"Mama and Daddy say he might've quit that job. Several times, he complained to them about the parents and principal at your school. Said they wouldn't let him alone to teach."

"I heard he cussed in his classes. I can't see any reason to cuss in a math class."

Luke tried out for the Stanly baseball team last year as a sophomore but didn't make it. Buck was coach of the team at the time. Luke didn't bother to try out again this year. He said he had enough to do with his schoolwork, his basketball, and his church softball. Truth be told, I think he harbors a grudge against Buck.

"Shoot, I've heard my own math teacher swear more than once this year when one of those snotnose boys from down on Crestmont Drive talked back to him in class," I said.

"I don't care how many teachers you've heard do it; that don't make it right." Luke doesn't curse or smoke. Nobody from out at his church does. "Look, Jonnie, let's change the subject. I've talked about Buck just about all I can stand."

I decided to drop the matter for the time being, but I wasn't through with it, not by a long shot. I changed the subject. "So JB's with that fake blonde from Landis tonight. Never dates one twice in a row, does he?"

"Ah, he just likes to play the field." Luke finds it easy to overlook faults in his buddies from the Tabernacle.

"How'd he meet her?"

"She and Cecilia came to a Friday Night Sing at our church back in February," he answered. "Cecilia introduced them."

"Oh, Cecilia was at the Sing too?"

Cecilia Shoe's daddy might be a Baptist preacher, but his daughter's just one step above a tramp. Mrs. Gilmore thinks no one can hold a candle to her when it comes to singing. She's always inviting her over from Charlotte to sing solos at the Tabernacle.

Somebody needs to tell her no one can hold a candle to Cecilia when it comes to certain other things too. Luke doesn't know it but Cecilia's got her eye on him. I've tried to tell him in a roundabout way, but he won't take the hint.

"Yes, Mrs. Gilmore invited her over to sing. She did a good job on "Though Your Sins Be as Scarlet," he said.

"How appropriate."

For a minute, I thought I'd gone too far but he let it go. My mama says I need to learn when to bite my tongue, but if Luke Goodman can't tell a cheap tramp when she stares him in the face, then I think somebody ought to give him some help.

I squinted once, twice. Tiny white flakes were touching down on the windshield.

"Oh look, Luke. It's snow!"

He frowned at the spring fields on the movie screen.

"No, not in the movie. Look outside." I pointed through my window. "Can you believe it?"

"Yeah, I see it. It's snow all right."

"Snow in March! Let's get out. Have you ever caught a snowflake on your tongue?"

"I thought you said you were cold," he replied.

"Look over there. Catherine Love's sitting on the hood of Lee Baucom's Chevy. Let's get out. C'mon." I moved toward my door but he cupped his chin in his palm.

"I hope the roads don't get slick," he mumbled. I've seen the same worry in his eyes when he's at my house around five on Sunday evening, and he remembers the Deliverance Tabernacle's youth meeting starts at five thirty.

"Snow in March with Easter just a few hours away. It's magic, that's what it is." I groped for the door handle again.

"I guess." He gazed toward the heavens but didn't move.

After that, I couldn't think of much else to say. We sat like two knots on a log for five or six minutes. Finally, the snow got me going again.

"Luke, look what it's doing to the windshield. It's like we're in some crystal cocoon. I could write a poem about it. I might do just that later on tonight."

"Listen, Jonnie, I don't want us to get stuck out here. You don't know how long it might keep up."

"Nobody else is leaving."

He looked from side to side and then at the rows of cars behind us. Most of the car windows had been fogged over for an hour or so, but snow had put sparkling blankets on top the fogged windshields. Our windshield wore the snow blanket, but unfortunately we'd been doing nothing that would cause our windows to fog up from the inside.

"Nobody else knows it's snowing," he replied. No smile.

I giggled. "Isn't that Eddie and Barb about ten rows up, close to the screen? Out beside the red Plymouth. They know it's snowing. He's trying to make a snowball. Come on, let's go down there."

"He's probably trying to clear his windshield so he can leave. I think we better get out of here while we can. I'm gonna clean off my windshield."

He asked for his sweater back and got out. I shivered both times he opened the door, getting out and getting back in. As we crept toward the exit sign, Pat Boone and Shirley Jones kissed on the screen. This time he didn't sing to her.

Luke had no trouble getting to my house, unless you count the time I slid over on his side of the car when we turned into Gibson Street. To tell the truth, that had nothing to do with the snow. It was only ten o'clock when we rolled down my driveway. We stood under my daddy's sixty-watt porch light for less than a minute before Luke bent to kiss me goodnight.

A laugh sounded across the empty field on the right of my house.

"What was that?" Luke asked.

"Sounds like some of Buck's ball players are over there," I said, nodding toward the dark outline of Buck's house just barely visible across the field. When Buck was a coach out at Stanly, his baseball players were crazy about him. Still are. After supper every Friday and sometimes on Saturday morning too, a carload of them pull up into his yard honking their horn and shouting. Buck brings out Pepsi Colas for them, and they sit on his front porch. Likely as not, they get up a ball game on the vacant lot. He usually pitches, a chaw of Brown's Mule stuffed in his jaw. Some of them chew too. He cusses a blue streak if one of them swings at a bad pitch or boots an easy grounder. It's been almost a year now since he left Stanly, but those same boys are still apt to show up on weekends.

"They got no business being over there this time of night," Luke said.

"You ever heard of a prayer meeting?" I replied.

No answer. Luke's not one to laugh at jokes about church things.

An eerie noise came from Buck's porch. It sounded a little like a hoot owl.

"Listen, I gotta go now," Luke said. "The snow might start back up again."

I let my middle finger trace the outline of his left ear.

The weird hoots came again, deeper than before. Then a gravely voice said, "Dick Tracy."

Other voices called out, "Whooo? Whooo?"

"Dick Tracy."

"Whooo? Whooo?"

"Luke Goodman. He's God's private dick."

While we stood watching, black shadows separated from the porch and disappeared into two cars in Buck's driveway. They didn't switch on their headlights or make any move to leave.

A chill went all over me. "Come in for a minute," I suggested. "They're giving me goose bumps."

"Jonnie, I really gotta go now. Call you next week." Luke bent just enough to brush his lips across mine and then jumped over the two porch steps to the sidewalk. His breath made icy little clouds until he ducked into his Ford.

It was just past ten when he left. Buck's ball players left shortly afterward. I've been sitting here at the kitchen table trying to get a poem started ever since. The words won't come, though, and the feeling's gone too. So I might as well have that last Moon Pie out of the cabinet and go on to bed.

Chapter 6

Seeing Red

On Easter morning about eight o'clock, I poked my head out the front door. Not one speck of snow was left. The air still felt chilly but nowhere near cold enough for more snow. Instead, the sky looked like we might get an April shower at any minute. Mama made Linda Sue and me add coats and umbrellas to our Easter outfits. We complained but she won out.

Sure enough, it started sprinkling as we drove down Gibson Street to church. Mama's umbrella didn't help the new permanent I gave her a couple weeks ago. I followed the directions on the Lilt box and it took pretty good, but the rain made it frizz this morning. She said she felt like Clarabelle the Clown. Daddy, Linda Sue, and I had gone in together to buy her a purple orchid corsage. Maybe a pretty hat would have been a better idea for this rainy morning.

The minute we stepped foot into the church, Linda Sue and I peeled off those winter jackets so people could see what we'd got for Easter. Linda Sue's dress was Carolina blue with a gathered bottom but not real full like the ones we used to put crinolines under. Instead of a hat, she took apart the gardenia corsage Daddy always gives us at Easter and used a bobby pin to fasten a flower over the rubber band that held her pony tail. I'll have to admit she looked good. If I was a blondie, I'd wear light blue every day.

Mama let me pick my own dress this year. I think it was about time. Last year when she took us to Belk's to choose Easter outfits, her face told me she didn't like a thing I put on. This year she gave me a twenty dollar bill, and I went straight to Catos, a store my mama wouldn't be caught dead in. I put on a white sack dress with bright blue pin stripes running up and down it and a white bucket hat made of straw. Nobody in my church had ever found the nerve to wear a sack dress on Sunday morning. I figured my slim figure would look good in one, so I might as well be the first.

At our house Daddy won't let us read the Sunday paper before church, but that doesn't mean the rest of Harmony follows any such rule. People in my Sunday School class were more interested in talking about Mrs. Gilmore's death than about Jesus' resurrection. I soon found out Sheriff Shepherd is looking for Red Byerly for questioning. Everybody knows I live beside Buck and asked me a dozen questions about him. I hate to admit it, but I enjoyed telling about seeing the deputy sheriff arrest him on Good Friday. I bet Linda Sue laid it on thick in her class too.

At last, Catherine Love took a minute to ask me where I'd found my cool sack dress. *Cool* is a word she uses, not me. You can't ask her the time of day without getting an answer with *cool* in it. Then she didn't give anybody else a chance to say they liked my dress before she asked why in the world Luke and I left the movie so early last night. I didn't answer real fast, so Eddie Walker chimed in talking about the snowball fight they had at the drive-in after we left.

I thought about announcing that my boyfriend insisted we leave early so we wouldn't get snowed in. I didn't though. They already think Luke's odd because you're more likely to find him at his church than up at the Hum Dinger. I don't know what they'd think if they knew he doesn't like to go to movies. He says people might get the wrong impression. They might think he approves of all the sex stuff you see in movies. Says he might to be a stumbling block for people who take him for an example. *Stumbling block.* Those are the very words he used one night last month right after we walked out of the Harmony Theater downtown. His words went down like a dose of medicine with me. It might've made more sense if we'd been at some Marilyn Monroe movie, but we'd just seen Kim Novac and Jimmy Stewart in *Vertigo*. That movie's meant to scare you, not to get you all hot and bothered.

In Sunday School, Sonny hung back and listened while people asked about the murder and the drive-in, but after church he walked up to me and eyed my Easter hat. He asked if it was a white paint bucket. When I didn't laugh, he changed the subject to Red Byerly. He wanted me to borrow Daddy's car so the two of us could go out looking for Red later in the day. For just a minute I was tempted. I couldn't figure out why Red had disappeared so close to the time Mrs. Gilmore was killed. For all anybody knew, he'd seen the murder. Worse yet, Mrs. Gilmore could have surprised him while he was stealing money from the church office and— I caught myself before my imagination ran wild.

Sonny's face fell a mile when I turned him down. I knew Mama would want the family to drive down in the country to Poplar Grove Cemetery to put flowers on Grandpa and Grandma Beech's and Grandma Sparks' graves like we do every year on Easter Sunday. That would take most of the afternoon. I hoped Sonny wouldn't jump on his bicycle and go out to Archie Byerly's house without me.

The sky opened and poured rain ten minutes after church let out, so Sonny's mama and little sister rode the half mile home with us. Daddy asked Sonny to ride too, but he said it was too crowded. On the way home Pearl—that's his mama—started talking about Buck. I considered telling her today would be a good day to make sure Sonny stayed home all afternoon. But then she's never had much control over him. Nobody has.

Right after lunch we were surprised when Buck's brother from Charlotte showed up on our front porch. George Eudy favors Buck in the face, and they're about the same size too. That's as far as it goes. He stood there in our doorway wearing a dark sport coat, gray slacks, a starched white shirt, and a nice tie. His outfit was a far cry from the dungarees or overalls we've seen Buck puttering around in seven days a week since he lost his teaching job. On days he's not scheduled to work over at the Tabernacle, he's likely to top his garb with just an old undershirt. Sometimes he wears scuffed-up brogans with high tops, but most of the time he doesn't bother to wear any shoes at all.

If I hadn't known George was Buck's brother, I'd have thought he was a Baptist preacher come to visit. I believe he's older than Buck but he didn't go to college. He sells used cars for a living, and his wife Bernice is a nurse at the big hospital over there in Charlotte. We know them well because they used to visit old Commodore Eudy and Miss Lillie every other week. George keeps bees as a hobby, and he used to bring us honey Bernice had put up in Mason jars. A couple years ago, he convinced Daddy to take on a swarm he'd cut down from a neighbor's tree in Charlotte, and Daddy's put up two more swarms himself since then. Daddy's honey is as good as George's always was, but I don't think Mama likes him climbing up his old stepladder to get swarms out of our neighbors' maples. Linda Sue and I didn't mind the first hive he put on the upper edge of his garden, but there's three sitting in a row now. During the summertime, you're taking a big risk to walk barefoot through the clovers in our back yard.

Daddy and George sat down in the living room. George pulled a pair of dark-rimmed glasses out of a pocket inside his jacket and put them on. They made his brown eyes look twice as big as Buck's little beady ones. He and Daddy started right in talking about Buck. Linda

63

Sue and I helped Mama clear the table, but as long as Daddy left the door between the living room and the kitchen open, we could hear most every word.

"I guess you and Lois are as shocked as Bernice and me are, John." I could tell George was embarrassed to have to come to Daddy like this.

"Yeah, we are. Jonnie and Linda Sue too. They saw the deputy come out here and get him Friday."

Mama banged the green bean pot against the frying pan, and I missed part of George's next sentence.

". . . the woman, and I don't think he did. He admits he left that church mad as all gitout but says he went straight home to sleep it off. Did any of y'all happen to see him come in Thursday night?"

"No, I don't think so. Lois and me woulda probably been in bed by the time he got home. I can't recollect hearing his old truck rattling." Daddy raised his voice. "Jonnie, you girls come in here a minute."

He didn't have to ask twice.

"George wonders if any of us heard Buck come home Thursday night. Probably around ten o'clock." Daddy looked straight at me.

"That's the night for *The Pat Boone Show*," I said. "We were watching it back in the den at nine o'clock. Then Mr. White had told my English class to watch that Ethan Frome thing on *Playhouse Ninety* at nine thirty. Mama let us stay up for it." I stopped and thought for a minute before I said, "But I don't remember any noises."

"Me neither, but we never hear Buck come or go unless it's summer and the windows are open," Linda Sue said.

"Why'd the sheriff wait until Friday to have Buck arrested if he was so sure he was the one who did the killing?" Daddy asked.

George nodded his head twice. "I asked that same thing myself," he said. "It seems Preacher Gilmore had mentioned that the Byerly boy sleeps in the church basement. The sheriff knew the boy had a jail record of sorts. He'd locked him up overnight a couple times when he found him drunk and disorderly."

"I'm afraid Red's goin' to end up as no count as his daddy," Daddy said.

"Sheriff Shepherd said he wants to question the boy as much as he wants to question Buck," George went on. "He's going to try to get some fingerprints off things in the basement and off Mrs. Gilmore's car too. He also wonders if there might be a connection between the murder and the broken tombstones in that little graveyard out near the Tabernacle. Y'all hear about vandals getting in there and messing it up here a while back?"

"Yeah, it was in *The Telegram*," Mama answered as she came into the living room holding one of the pots I was supposed to be drying.

"The girls had me call a deputy about Red on Friday night," Daddy said. "They thought the Tabernacle's softball players might have forgot to tell the sheriff about him sleepin' in the basement."

65

"Well, he's still loose, so there's not been any questioning yet."

"You want to know the real reason Sheriff Shepherd waited so long to arrest anybody?" I asked Daddy.

Linda Sue raised her palm to her forehead and closed her eyes. "Here it comes," she said in a shaky, spooky voice. "Jonnie's using her ESP."

"ESP's got nothing to do with it," I said. "I just know Sheriff Shepherd's son Shay played baseball for Buck a couple years ago. He was good. Stanly High hasn't had anything like him since. When he graduated, Buck saw to it that he got a scholarship to State College. He's in Raleigh right now, going to school and playing ball. The sheriff was like us, Daddy. He didn't want Buck sitting in no jail."

"You're probably right there, Jonnie," Daddy said.

George stared at his lap and tapped the fingers of his right hand on his thigh. He didn't look up for the longest time. The quiet made me uneasy.

"Well, I guess we're going to have to get Buck a lawyer pretty quick," he said finally. "They're just holding him for questioning right now. Course, it's murder they're trying to pin on him."

"And if they do," Mama said, "they won't let him out on bond."

"Wonder if Clayton Wilkie would take his case? He used to handle most of my daddy's business," George said.

"I don't know if he takes murder cases," Daddy said. "Fact is, I can't remember the last murder case we had in Harmony. You can't count Rose Byerly. They never caught the one who shot her, so there was no call for a lawyer."

"You ought to try Lawyer Wilkie, George," Mama said. "He's a mighty fine man. Helps John and me with our taxes every year, and he don't charge you an arm and a leg either. He's done lots of work for people down at the mill. Lets them make payments as they get the money. He'd treat Buck right."

"I'll be back over here tomorrow morning then," George said, "and I'll have Bernice make a withdrawal from our bank account. After this last year, I doubt Buck has much of his savings left."

George looked over at Linda Sue and then at me. "Girls," he said, "I need to ask you to feed Willie for Buck while he's gone. I'll pay you, of course."

"We already thought of that," Linda Sue said. "Mama's let us take him the table scraps the last two nights."

"They've always liked old Willie," Mama said. "They'll be glad to help out." She threw us a quick smile and then looked back at George. "And don't go talking about pay. As good as your mama and daddy always were to my little girls—" She let her voice trail off.

"I thank you all for your help. There's one more favor I want to ask of you, John. Could you give me directions to Archie Byerly's house? If his boy disappeared the same night Mrs. Gilmore was killed, it looks mighty suspicious. I don't know the details but it won't hurt for me to ask Archie about it."

"Why don't I just go out there with you," Daddy offered.

I had to think fast. "Daddy, you ought to let me go too," I said.

"Jonnie, you ain't got no more business out there than the man in the moon."

"But Daddy, Red's just a couple years older than me. I've seen him plenty of times out at Luke's church. If he should turn up at his daddy's, he might come closer to talking to me than to y'all. The two of you could go up and talk to Archie, and I'll—"

"All right, Jonnie, you can go, but you're going to stay in the car while me and George go up to the house. You hear?"

"Yes, Daddy, and you're right. I'll stay in the car and I'll keep the doors locked." I knew not to push him any further. Not right then anyway.

Linda Sue stood beside Mama, her eyes as popped as a toady frog's and her mouth open so wide that her whole pony tail could've fit inside it. Any other time she would've pitched a fit to go too, but this time she couldn't come up with a single reason to tag along. We headed for Archie Byerly's place without her.

When we pulled up beside the house, a pile of skinny dogs untangled themselves and came out from under the only shade tree on the property. I counted fourteen. Most of them were some kind of mix, black with brown splotches and long bony legs. Four or five were little white fices with liver-colored spots marking their faces. They barked like they were ready to tear us apart, but when Daddy stomped his foot at them, they scattered. Within five minutes of the time Daddy and George stepped inside Archie's door, every one of them had lifted his leg to pee on George's tires. I'd meant to do a little exploring, but I was afraid to get out of the car after they got to stirring. Who's to say one of them wouldn't have lifted his leg on me.

It didn't take long for me to get bored sitting there by myself. The rain had stopped but the sky was full of gray clouds. I cracked my window a couple inches to get some air and must have dropped off to sleep. I was in the middle of a dream where I was sitting in Luke's car at the Starlite Drive-in. I was by myself and had fallen asleep. Someone was tapping on my window. When I opened my eyes in the dream, it was Pat Boone and he wanted me to get out of the car. I reached for the door handle but woke up and saw Red Byerly's big freckled face staring through the window. His green eyes couldn't hold a candle to Pat's blue ones.

"Hurry up, Jonnie," he said in a loud whisper through the crack. "I don't want your daddy coming out and finding me standing here."

"Red, you scared me. Do you know the sheriff's looking for you?"

"Course I do," he snorted. "You think I been on Mars?"

"Just where *have* you been?" I shot back at him.

"Get outta that car," he growled.

"Not till you answer my question. And you'd be better off if you talked to somebody about your whereabouts on Thursday night."

"You're right. I need to talk to somebody and you'll do until I can get to my old man. Come on." He yanked the car door open, and half a dozen hounds began sniffing my legs. Red cussed and bent down to slap them out of the way. He took my arm and pulled me toward a wooden building that was missing part of its tin roof and looked like it'd never had a lick of paint.

I wasn't sure I wanted to be in an old barn with a boy who'd disappeared the same night Mrs. Gilmore was killed. Fact is, I was scared. He opened the door and pushed me inside before I could make up my mind to argue with him. A couple stalls covered one wall. I guess somebody kept horses or maybe a mule there at one time, but now the stall doors needed repair and there wasn't a sign of any animals but dogs. Archie's pack of hounds must sleep in the barn. Maybe not all the time but enough to leave their smell.

Another odor almost covered the dog smell. I wrinkled my nose and squinted in the dim light trying to figure out what it was. Like the outside, the inside walls had never seen the first coat of paint. But opposite the stalls, Archie had built three rows of shelves, and paint can after paint can lined them. Every size, every color, every brand. If the place hadn't been such a total mess, it could've passed for a paint store. White, blue, and yellow paint globs rolled down the sides of cans. Some had lids but wooden stirrers stuck out the tops of others. The paint inside them was probably dry as overcooked grits. A small can of red lay on its side with no lid in sight. Was that dried paint in the puddle beside it? Or maybe blood? The Nancy Drew mysteries Mama gave me on birthdays and Christmases whispered to me: "*Murder in the Old Barn.*" I swallowed hard and managed to grin at my imagination.

"Turn loose of my arm before you make a bruise on it," I told Red.

He lowered his brows and scrunched his fat lips into a frown but let me go. After a few seconds, he grunted, "Sorry."

I took a look back through the big door Red had left open. Satisfied we'd see Daddy and George when they came out of Archie's house, I started right in on him. "Red, I can't understand why you're hiding." He didn't answer, just cut his eyes around the barn like he thought Tubby Shepherd might jump out of a horse stall at any minute.

"Unless you're guilty." I caught and held his eyes.

"You know I didn't kill her," he said. "They've already got the killer in jail. That crazy Buck Eudy."

"What about the person who painted ugly pictures of Mrs. Gilmore on the back of the church about a month ago?" My eyes moved to the rows of paint cans lining the wall.

"What about it?" he answered. "Could've been any kid in the county. I wouldn't put it past the Peacock twins to have painted them. That kinda trick would tickle them good."

"I've heard Buck wasn't the only person who couldn't get along with Mrs. Gilmore. Didn't she cross some of the members of the congregation too?"

"Church gossip." He made a noise that was half laugh and half snort. "She pointed her finger and spoke her mind. Sometimes it bothered the ones she pointed at but not enough to make anybody go and murder her."

"So you don't think the killer is a church member?"

"Sure don't. It'd take a crazy person to kill a preacher's wife." He tapped his index finger on the side of his head. "You live beside Buck. Don't tell me you haven't noticed he's been a little bit off the last year or so. That's why he's a janitor in a church instead of a baseball coach in a high school these days."

I let his remarks pass for the time being and got back to Red himself. "You ever think how suspicious it looks for you to disappear right after Mrs. Gilmore was killed? Why haven't you gone on in to answer the sheriff's questions?"

"I intend to do just that now that the sheriff has his killer all locked up tight. If I'd turned up to sleep at the church Thursday night, it mighta been me he arrested." He picked up a paint brush and began hitting it against the rotten wall. I wished I was back out in the light of day, even if it meant fighting off the yapping dogs.

"What I want to know before I rush into anything is how much evidence they got on Buck," Red said, still banging the brush.

"Sheriff Shepherd's keeping his lip zipped about the whole case," I said. "But it's just been three days. He may know more any day now."

"So, the sheriff made his arrest mainly on what Billy Mack Barrier, Grady Peacock, and your boyfriend told him about the trouble Buck caused after the cookout. That right?" He threw the paint brush across the barn into an empty stall.

I tried to pretend he hadn't startled me. "Yes," I said, "as far as I know. Were you at the church when Buck threw down the broom and stomped out of the basement?"

"No, I read it in today's paper. I just went to that cookout to eat the hot dogs. If you ask me, that whole softball team's a drag. Think they're such big wheels just because they score runs in a church league."

Whether he meant to or not, he was putting down my boyfriend. "Not everybody can be on a school team," I said quickly. "Have you ever been on one?"

"Maybe I have." He folded his arms across his chest and puffed out his cheeks. I knew one thing for sure. He wasn't on any kind of team now.

"It ain't baseball they're playing," he said. "It's softball. Grady and Parks Peacock prance around the bases like a couple of tooth fairies." He raised his right hand to the paint shelf and made his fingers prance down it before he added, "JB Blanton's the only thing they got close to a real player, and I hear he's 'bout quit showing up."

"If you weren't at the cookout for the whole party, where were you?"

His brows furrowed like he might give me a sharp answer but he didn't. "I went to the cookout, but as soon as I had my fill of food, I left for Black Bottom. I had me some beer hid in the woods down there. Put it there after Mrs. Gilmore gave me a place to sleep on the condition that I stay clear of strong drink. I laid up against a pine tree and drunk the whole six pack"

"You fell off the wagon?"

"Yep. I shore did."

"So when did you hear about Mrs. Gilmore?"

73

"I went back to the church that night intending to sleep there like always. Got there 'bout eleven o'clock, but didn't pull into the parking lot because there was a brown patrol car sitting in it. The church was all lit up too. I was half drunk but sober enough to know to stay clear of whatever was going on. I parked my truck down the road and hid in the woods to watch. The deputy musta been inside the building. The preacher and the sheriff was sitting on the curb near the Gilmores' blue Plymouth. The car trunk was open. I figured some hoodlum had broke into it looking for something to steal." Red's voice got shaky and his hands did too. "Guess the ambulance had done got Mrs. Gilmore."

I wondered if Red really cared about Mrs. Gilmore or if this was just an act he was putting on for me.

"Wasn't long before I knew I was watching something bigger than a burglary investigation," he went on. "The Reverend was pretty broke up. The sheriff was trying to ask him questions, but sometimes he'd bury his head in both his hands like it was all he could do to hold it up. Then Elder Humpy Barrier and his wife showed up to help the preacher. Billy Mack was with them, ready to put in his two cents worth."

A couple of the little fices stuck their heads through the crack in the barn door and yapped. "Git on outta here," Red growled and pushed them with a foot that was bigger than either one of them.

"I already told you I was half drunk. I knew it wouldn't do for the Law to find me there in that shape," he continued. "Besides, sometimes it seems like I'm the only sinner over at that church."

I grinned and said, "I know the feeling. It's risky for me to go over there with Luke. I might wind up part of the next sermon."

Red looked at me like he didn't believe me and then checked to see if the men were still occupied in the house. "Most of that bunch is like people out of some story in the Bible," he said. "I knew I'd be the first one they blamed for whatever had went wrong that night."

"What did you do next?"

"Got back in my truck real quiet like and backed it up a piece. I turned around at a wide place in the road and drove back to Black Bottom. That's where I've been ever since, hiding in the same woods where they found my mama's body five years ago. Swiped a *Telegram* out of a yard Friday evening and found out what had happened to Mrs. Gilmore. Saturday when all the colored people went to town, I slipped into a woman's kitchen and took me a bowl of pinto beans and a hunk of cornbread. Swiped a Sunday *Telegram* off a porch this morning when the colored people were at their Sunrise Service. Seeing how the sheriff's got Buck in jail now, I guess it's safe for me to come out. What you think?"

"Go talk to Sheriff Shepherd," I said quickly. Then I thought of another possibility. "And go talk to Rev. Gilmore. He could use some company in the house right now and the church has lost a janitor. You could move in and take on that job, at least for the time being."

"Yeah, you might be right about the job. I'll think about it. But I ain't interested in boarding at the preacher's house.. I'd rather just keep on sleeping on the cot Mrs. Gilmore put in the church basement when she first took an interest in me." He put his hand over his mouth and held his chin for a minute. "Yeah, think I'll do just that. I got unfinished business at that church anyway."

Before I had time to wonder about the unfinished business, he went on. "Thanks, for catching me up, Jonnie. Now, I won't need to talk to my old man. Listen to him rant and rave at me."

"Don't mention it." I smiled to myself. Red hadn't learned any more from me than I had from him.

"There's one more thing I want to ask you about." Red looked down at the barn's dirt floor and scratched the back of his neck. Then he shook his head back and forth real slow like he didn't know whether to say anything else or not. I just waited for him to make up his mind.

"Since you been dating Luke Goodman," he finally said, "you probably know more about the Tabernacle than a lot of people in Harmony."

"Maybe," I answered and shrugged my shoulders.

"Well, you ever noticed anything kinda funny going on, anything that made you wonder?"

I blushed..

"You have, Jonnie. Own up to it."

"No," I lied. But I thought about the scene I witnessed out at their day camp last summer and hoped Red couldn't read my mind. "What're you talking about anyway?" I said.

"Sometimes it seems like Rev. Gilmore gets some kinda charge outta—" he began. We heard a screen door slam just then and saw George and Daddy start down Archie's rickety porch steps.

"I got to go, Red. I promised Daddy I wouldn't get out of the car. You go to the sheriff, like I said." I slipped out of the barn before he could say another word.

Chapter 7

The Good Daddy

My daddy doesn't smoke cigarettes just like he doesn't drink liquor. Oh, he might have a hot toddy on Christmas Eve, but he's never been one to smoke. George Eudy cranked his shiny '58 Olds and aimed it back toward town. I saw him fumble in the pocket of his white shirt and come out with a pack of Chesterfields. He held it in his one free hand and tapped it on the steering wheel. Two cigarettes popped up in the square opening and he reached the pack across to Daddy. "John?" he said.

"Believe I will," Daddy answered. I wonder if he knew how big my eyes got when he took one of the two cigarettes. George stretched his arm up to the dashboard and pushed in the cigarette lighter. I sat in the back seat afraid my daddy would make a fool of himself trying to smoke that Chesterfield. He didn't though. In fact, he managed it just like he'd smoked a pack a day for most of his thirty-six years. It made me uneasy.

"You reckon that old sot is trying to make an alibi for his boy?" Daddy asked after his first puff.

"That must be it, John. I can't think of any other reason he'd put himself at the scene of that awful murder."

I couldn't hold still another minute. "What did Archie say?" I butted in.

Daddy jerked around in his seat and stared at me hard before he answered. He blew out a stream of blue Chesterfield smoke. I swear he looked like Jeff Chandler. Mama says I got Daddy's wavy black hair and big eyes and that's the reason she gave me his name. I guess I could've done worse.

Daddy coughed and stubbed his cigarette out in George's ashtray. I think he'd forgot I was in the back seat. But then he surprised me. "George, you mind if I tell Jonnie?"

"No reason not to," answered George. "Archie said he's already told Sheriff Shepherd."

I saw that same sparkle in Daddy's blue eyes that I see when Linda Sue and I get him to talking about ghosts or UFO"S. If Mama's around, she'll say, "John, I'd just as soon you leave such subjects alone," but Daddy likes to talk about strange things as much as us girls do.

"He says he hasn't seen Red since the murder," said Daddy, "but Archie hisself was over at the Tabernacle Thursday night right about the time Mrs. Gilmore got killed. Least that's his story, and he says Red was nowhere around the church at that time. Nobody was."

"But what business would Archie have going over there between nine and ten o'clock at night? He isn't even a member of that church," I said.

"Or any church, for that matter," Daddy added. "According to him, Red made forty dollars helping Humpy Barrier paint his house last week. He told us Red owed him part of it for past rent and board, so he went to the Tabernacle to collect that night."

"And you think he might be trying to give Red an alibi for the night?" I leaned forward toward the front seat.

"It's what a daddy would do if he's any good," said George Eudy. His voice was as steady and kind as his own daddy's, Commodore Eudy's, had been.

Daddy stuck his lips out and brought his eyebrows so low they almost touched his long eyelashes. "George, we ain't talking 'bout just any daddy here," he said. "We're talking 'bout Archie Byerly. This is a feller who raised a stink when Mrs. Gilmore decided she'd try to straighten out Red the night he busted into a Tabernacle prayer meeting drunk. I guess you never heard 'bout that."

George hadn't. Daddy's always glad to tell a good story. He gave George the wild tale I had brought home from Luke, the one where Red was looking for his mama that night at the prayer meeting. The part that interested George most was how mad Archie got when

Mrs. Gilmore took Red in and gave him a place to sleep in the church basement, not just that one night, but every night since up until the murder.

"One thing's for sure," George said, "my brother's not the only one who looks suspicious here. At least, he says he was home at the time the murder took place. Archie Byerly, on the other hand, admits he was right there at the Tabernacle, and you say he's holding a grudge against the Gilmores."

"Then there's the boy hisself," Daddy added. "Where's he been since Mrs. Gilmore was killed? He's liable to know something about the murder." He twisted his neck around to look at me. "I told George about calling the sheriff last night to let him know Red had been sleeping at the church."

There was my chance. I found the nerve to tell them about my long talk with Red in the barn and made sure George understood Red had promised to go to the sheriff.

"So, that's two of the Byerlys who were at the scene of the murder." George sounded like he'd just found his dark-rimmed bifocals after having to read without them for days. "Wonder how they missed seeing each other?"

"Red said he didn't go back to the church to sleep that night until around eleven. That would've been after the murder," I reminded him.

Daddy nodded to agree with me. "And according to Archie's story," he added, "there weren't no signs of commotion at the Tabernacle at the time he passed through. Least not till *he* got there.

81

He's been known to cause right much commotion hisself when he's two sheets to the wind. When his wife Rose was alive, I heard tell they had some real commotion out at their house."

Daddy caught himself and didn't go any further. Again, he'd almost forgot it was his daughter in the back seat.

George put his hand up to the side of his clean-shaven face. "John," he said, "I wonder if I could trouble you to drive me to the sheriff's office? I need you to verify the things I discuss with him."

Daddy dropped me at home before he and George Eudy went to talk to Sheriff Shepherd. I couldn't think up any good arguments to get him to take me along, so I decided to let well enough alone. After all, I was the first person to talk to Red Byerly since he disappeared last Thursday night..

While we were at Archie's, Mama and Linda Sue delivered Easter daffodils to Grandma Sparks' and Grandma and Grandpa Beech's graves. I'd just begun telling them about Archie Byerly's pack of peeing dogs when Sonny Calloway spun his bicycle down our driveway. Sometimes I think he sees himself as Fireball Roberts and his Schwinn as a hot racecar. For his sake I started the whole story over. Mama listened without saying much at all, but Sonny and Linda Sue asked so many questions I had a hard time keeping the story going.

At the end Sonny frowned and said, "I wish I'd known you were going out there. I think I coulda got more out of Red."

I tried not to laugh in his face. He was just talking out of jealousy. If he hadn't been there to make such remarks, Linda Sue would've said the same things and for the same reason.

* * * *

On Easter Sunday most people go eat lunch at their grandparents' house after church. Easter Sundays don't go exactly that way at my house. Both my grandmas are dead. I never saw either one of them alive, much less ate Easter lunch with them. Mama tells about sneaking me into Stanly Memorial Hospital when her daddy had his heart attack. She says I stood beside his bed and played with his big fingers, but I was only two years old at the time. Much as I'd like to do it, I can't honestly say that I remember Grandpa Beech.

I do have one grandpa left alive, my daddy's daddy. When Grandpa Sparks was young, he used to farm several acres each year for one big farm owner or another in Anson County, where Daddy grew up. Mama says Daddy had a rough time back then because his daddy always let every penny that came his way slip right on through his fingers. Now that he's old, he gets a check in the mail once a month. It goes the same way his pennies used to go.

Holidays are likely to be his worst times. He lives with his second wife and two boarders in an old two-story frame house in China Grove. We visit him once a month on Sunday afternoon, but that's the last place we'd show up to eat on Easter Sunday. When we do visit, Mama reminds Linda Sue and me not to touch anything and to keep our hands out of our mouths until we can get home to wash them. If they ever offered anything to eat—which they never do—we'd be scared to take it unless it was in a cellophane wrapper.

Easter lunch at my house is nothing out of the ordinary. Mama gets up Sunday morning at 6 AM and puts on a big pot roast or fries a chicken just like she does every other Sunday before we go to church. Then we eat it when we come home.

Now, I'm not saying my mama would let a holiday go by without doing something a little special. After George Eudy and Daddy got back from the sheriff's office and George was on his way home to Charlotte, Mama put her hand on Daddy's shoulder and asked him if he'd get the grill out from under the house and cook some hamburgers. He agreed and Mama told Sonny he was welcome to eat supper with us. Grilling hamburgers is something that doesn't happen at his house, so he was quick to say yes and offer to help Daddy. While he and Daddy went looking for the grill, Linda Sue brought folding lawn chairs out of the car shed and I found a brush to scrub the grill top.

"Hey, Jonnie," Sonny said as I worked, "you never got around to telling me about the evening you went out to the Tabernacle's day camp to collect your boyfriend."

I threw a look at Linda Sue and said, "Aw, that story's nothing compared to one Daddy can tell about a Tabernacle meeting back when they didn't even have a building on their land. They were holding a revival in what they used to call a brush arbor. I don't think Daddy was some kind of fanatic, but for some reason he and his

84

brother decided to go out in the country to this revival on a Saturday night."

Sonny and Linda Sue's eyes left me and stuck like magnets on something just behind my head. Sonny punched me and Linda Sue giggled. I had turned halfway around before my daddy started speaking. "You're right, Jonnie, I wasn't no kind of religious fanatic." The twinkle in his big blue eyes told me he'd enjoyed surprising me.

"Me and your Uncle Curly were just teenagers." he went on. "We were curious and looking for a good time. There weren't no television back then, and we didn't have money to go to a picture show. Besides, there were usually some pretty girls sitting on the back row at the revival meetings. Fact, two of the McClamrock sisters had promised to save us a seat that night."

I was relieved when Daddy took up the story. Like as not, Sonny would forget Linda Sue's comment about what I'd seen out at the Tabernacle's day camp last August. At least I hoped so.

"As I recall," Daddy continued, "we got there late that night and had took us a little snort of whiskey on the way. We could hear them singing long before we ever got down the hill to the brush arbor."

"The brush arbor?" Sonny interrupted.

Daddy frowned at him. "Yeah, back in them days when a church wanted a cool place to hold their revivals in the summertime, they went way out in the country and put up some rough timbers and laid branches and broom straw on the top to keep the weather out. The

85

sides were open and they had lanterns hanging all around inside to light it up at night."

"How old did you say you and Uncle Curly were?" Linda Sue asked.

"Well, it was eighteen or twenty years ago. I reckon we'd been close to eighteen years old. We weren't the only ones to go out there. They always got a good crowd on Friday and Saturday nights.

"This particular night Sylvester Kizer was preaching. He worked down at the mill in the daytime and preached on the side. He was the youngest of Zeb Kizer's boys. They all took after their no-count daddy, but Sylvester had gotten off of liquor and was trying to be a preacher now. He was skinny as a dogwood and bout as bumpy. I'll say one thing for him though. He could preach circles around the Methodist preachers in Harmony. Had the women wringing their hands and tears streaming down their faces every night. Not many meetings passed without somebody or other getting what they called the Holy Ghost and rolling around on the ground too."

I nudged Sonny. "Didn't I tell you the Tabernacle is full of strange people?"

Daddy's face got serious and he took up his story again. "But anyway, that night 'bout the time Sylvester was winding up his sermon, I saw a light in the east way high over his head. It looked to be miles away but kept growing and finally just lit up the sky."

Sonny's eyebrows shot up.

"Well, I got kind of uncomfortable," Daddy said. "Course everybody else saw it too. They was all squirming and saying things under their breath."

Daddy poured charcoal into the grill and saturated it with charcoal lighter. He bent and held a kitchen match close to the little black bricks. Flames flew up with a whoosh.

"Sylvester, he turned around and looked over his shoulder toward the east," Daddy said. "In a minute he faced us again and his eyes were as big as the ones on them praying mantises. He threw his long arms in the air and yelled, 'Lord God! Jesus is coming. Let's go meet Him.'

"Then he started running up the hill in the direction of that blazing light, motioning for the crowd to follow after him. Some of them did just that. Me, I wanted to get out of there and I did."

Daddy laughed at his own story and we laughed with him.

Mama came down the breezeway steps with a plate of hamburger patties. "I want you to know I wasn't one of the girls who sat beside your daddy that night," she said.

"Nah, but me and Curly took them McClamrock girls home early and went back over to Hub's Cafe close to midnight. Cleg Sides was over there sipping liquor out of a bottle in a paper sack and chasing it with Co'cola. He asked us, 'Where you two spark plugs been this time of night?' He liked to play around with our name like that.

"We said, 'Nowhere much.'

"Then he told us, 'I just thought you might've been out there where the mail plane fell near Shakespear Harris's farm. Sent out a bunch of flares as it went down.'"

Mama finished his story. "So that's the night John Sparks saw the light," she said, "and it was in a brush arbor with the McClamrock sisters from the Deliverance Tabernacle." Daddy lowered his head to hide his grin, but Sonny, Linda Sue, and I laughed out loud.

Sonny gave his seat to Mama and took her plate of patties. He and Daddy managed to let the littlest hamburger slip through the grill's open slots and into the fire. By that time though, Willie had smelled the grilling and made his way across Buck's vacant field hoping for supper. Sonny swore the dog grinned when he threw him the burned hamburger.

The sun set before the hamburgers were done. The March air was too cool for us to eat in the backyard, so the five of us moved into the kitchen to eat our supper and talk about the murder.

Daddy said George Eudy had told the sheriff about Archie and Red Byerly being at the Tabernacle the night of the murder. Sheriff Shepherd plans to question both of them.

"He told us he hates to have to hold Buck on this murder charge, seeing that he's never been arrested before in his life," Daddy said between bites of hamburger. "But he thinks Buck was the only one who had any cause to murder Mrs. Gilmore. He said he'd heap rather have either one of the Byerlys locked up than have Buck in jail right now. Neither one of them would be a stranger to a jail cell."

Daddy's words made my stomach feel funny. Red sure hadn't acted like a murderer in the barn today. I hope he beats the sheriff to the draw and goes in on his own to tell what he knows. If he's innocent, that is

"But Daddy," I said, "Red didn't try to hide it from me that he was at the Tabernacle just after the police found the body."

"I know what he told you, Jonnie, but you can't just take his word as the Gospel truth. He ain't got nobody to back up his story. Sheriff Shepherd might get something out of him that the boy didn't want to tell you."

Linda Sue was quick to agree. "Yeah, Jonnie, how do you know Red's not lying through his teeth?"

"It's goin' to take some time for the whole truth to come out," Mama nodded.

"I just don't want the same thing happening to Red that happened to Buck last Friday," I said. "Red doesn't have a brother like George Eudy to get him a lawyer and search for holes in the sheriff's evidence."

Sonny looked over at me. "No," he said, "but it looks like he's got you."

His look made my skin crawl. I scrambled off my chair and started cleaning up the table. My mama was more surprised than anybody else when I picked up the first dish. She started to help but I pushed her away and said, "Come on, Linda Sue. You've got ten fingers just like me."

"And you're the pot to call the kettle black," she said.

Mama and Daddy moved off to the den to tune in *The Jack Benny Show*, one of their favorite TV programs. Sonny brought his empty plate and tea glass over to the sink and handed them to me.

"Why don't you pitch in and rinse the things Jonnie washes," Linda Sue suggested. "Then I'll dry them and put them up."

He agreed too fast, and it was only a matter of seconds before I knew why.

"Y'all might think I've forgotten what you almost told me about Good-Man Luke's church camp." He curved his mouth up into a fake grin. "But I ain't. So what you say? Let's have it, Jonnie."

A white coffee cup slipped out of Linda Sue's hand and clattered onto the pile of plates in the rinse sink. I just kept right on moving the soapy dishrag up and down over the forks and spoons and trying to figure a way to get out of telling something Luke had made me promise to keep my mouth shut about. I put the last silverware into the rinse sink and let the wash water drain out of mine. Then I reached for the hand towel and turned to face Sonny while I dried my hands.

"Right now, there're just three things you need to know about that story," I said. I tilted my head back a little so I was looking down my nose at him. "Number one is that my little sister with the big mouth had no business mentioning it to you at all. Number two is that if I ever get ready to talk to anybody about it, I—not Linda Sue—will let you know. Number three is that the very next time you decide to try asking me about it, you're going to lose your rides up to the Hum-Dinger, your hamburgers off our grill, and maybe the best friend you've got on Gibson Street." I lowered my head and my voice. "You understand?" I said.

"Got it," he answered without looking up from the rinse water in his sink.

Chapter 8

The Bulldog

John and Lois Sparks sent me a client today. I've filled out their tax forms for years, along with those of half the good people who work in C. A. Davidson's mills. The salt of the earth. They're that all right, but they don't have much spare cash to spend on legal fees.

This client is not looking for somebody to fill out his tax forms. Buck Eudy is accused in the shocking murder case my wife Maizie first brought home from the beauty shop Friday afternoon. At one time he taught and coached at a county high school. More recently, he's been doing janitorial work at the Deliverance

Tabernacle of Faith and repairing clocks for folks in Harmony. John and Lois sent his brother to my office looking for someone to defend the accused in court. I knew he needed a criminal lawyer from Charlotte or Raleigh and told the brother so up front. He explained, and I have no doubt of the truth of his statement, that Buck couldn't afford a big city lawyer.

I've handled a dozen or so criminal cases in my thirty-three years of practicing law in Harmony. Just one of them was a murder case. A tiny woman who worked in Harmony Mills got tired of her drunken husband beating on her one Friday nights and shot him three times, twice in the belly and once in the chest. Her two little boys witnessed the whole thing and verified every word of her story. She never had to do a single day in prison. I'm afraid constructing a defense for this man won't be as easy as that one was.

Buck comes from a good family. Old Commodore Eudy was one of four siblings. For some reason or other, their parents gave every one of them a military name: Commodore, Sergeant, Major, and General. Lucky none of them were women. When their daddy died, the brothers inherited his farm land and lived off the real estate business the rest of their lives.

Textile executive C. A. Davidson purchased a large portion of that land from Sergeant, Major, and General Eudy for mere pennies back in the 20's, but Commodore refused to sell him any of his. He knew Davidson planned to build rent houses around Plant 6 in Harmony like he'd done around Plant 2 in Davidsonville several years before. That way, he could keep his labor force near his mill and make a little money off the rent he collected as well. Commodore said the company had too much control in workers' lives, and the Strike of 1934 proved him correct. Many of the poor men and women who picketed for higher wages that year never saw the inside of Harmony Mills again.

I've heard tell that Commodore's youngest son Buck (I wonder what his real name is) is natured like his Daddy—independent and outspoken. Maizie's niece Sylvia, whom we took to church and lunch yesterday, told us she was a member of his algebra class at Stanly High School four or five years ago. She said she'd never had any complaint about him but some folks had. Oh, she admitted he sometimes cursed when a kid went to sleep in class, and she'd seen him throw erasers at misbehaving boys. But she said she'd rather have a weird teacher than a boring one. I guess he finally threw an eraser at a family name that failed to tolerate colorful forms of discipline.

Yesterday, Maizie pled her case like a cross between a lawyer and a mother, trying to persuade Sylvia to stop working at that church. And she won too. Sylvia gave up playing the piano for choir practices and services at the Tabernacle, at least until the murder case is solved.

I'm going over to the county jail to talk with this Buck Eudy, and chances are I'll take his case unless it's obvious that he's guilty. Tonight at supper, Mazie may direct some of the same arguments at me that she directed at her niece yesterday. She'll probably add that I'm too old for this kind of case. When she sees she's going to lose this time, she'll shake her head and tell me I'm a sucker for an

94

underdog. But then she'll remember the lessons she used to teach in her American Government classes at Harmony High School and reach across the table to squeeze my hand and wink.

We get along.

* * * *

Neither my conversation with George Eudy this morning nor the *weird* Sylvia used to describe her former teacher yesterday prepared me for my initial interview with Buck Eudy. He rose from the side of his bunk when the guard let me into his cell, and I began as I would have with any prospective client.

"Mr. Eudy, my name is Clayton Wilkie. I am a lawyer and your brother George asked me to talk with you and consider defending you in court. May I sit down?" I gestured at a straight-backed chair and then moved to it and sat down.

"You work for the government?" He reseated himself on the edge of his bunk. His tiny eyes darted from me to the four corners of his cell like he thought somebody might be hiding in one of them to listen.

"No, my practice is here in Harmony. Your father consulted me once on a lawsuit C. A. Davidson was considering bringing against him back in the late 1940's."

Buck looked toward the ceiling. "I didn't hear a helicopter."

"Pardon?"

"How'd you get here?"

"My office is across Church Street and down a block. I walked over."

"You ever work in Washington?"

"No, I've lived in Harmony most of my sixty years. I spent time at college in Chapel Hill, North Carolina, and a year in France during the First World War, but I've never lived in Washington. Why do you ask?"

"You got a face like Winston Churchill, that British fellow President Roosevelt used to talk to during the war."

I laughed. "Well, I didn't play any part in World War II, but one of our county judges did nickname me Bulldog. I'd have to consider Churchill a step up."

My God, this man's eyes are no bigger than midget brown marbles, and his nose looks like it might've been hit by a hanging curve ball back when he coached baseball. His whiskers can't decide what color they want to be, black or white. Where did he come up with the nerve to compare my face to Churchill's? Lucky he doesn't know I like cigars.

"Now about the case," I continued. "You have been accused of murdering Eunice Faye Gilmore on the night of Thursday, March 28, between 9 and 10:15 PM. Where were you during that time period?"

He pointed a long, skinny finger at me. "You're bound to be one of the FBI agents they been sending down here to watch me since I told the school board what they could do with their teaching job at

Stanly High School. You can ask me questions till you're blue in the face, Mister, but I'm not telling you a thing."

"Mr. Eudy, I've never been connected to the FBI. Your brother George came over here from Charlotte this morning to meet with me and ask me to represent you in court. I was recommended to him by your neighbors, Lois and John Sparks. Your brother left my office at 10:30 on his way over here. Didn't he tell you I was coming to talk with you this afternoon?"

"Maybe he did." He scratched his whiskers. "You know Lois and John?"

"I've done legal work for them ever since they got married and moved up there on Gibson Street. I filled out their tax forms two weeks ago. I do it every year."

"They're good neighbors. Good people." He dropped his eyes to his feet. "But I think two FBI fellers were trying to question John about me one Saturday morning when he was out there working in the shrubbery beside his house. They came up dressed in white shirts and black pants. Disguised. Both had fistfuls of papers but they didn't fool me."

"Sounds like Jehovah's Witnesses," I said. "Didn't they come to your door too?"

"Sure did. They knocked and knocked, but I'd locked it and turned off my radio. I saw through their disguises and I had no intention of having anything to do with them. Jehovah's Witnesses? That's horse manure."

"Well, you're going to have to answer some questions before I decide whether or not I want to take your case. You were employed at the Deliverance Tabernacle, weren't you?"

"I worked out there some." His eyes rested on me while he answered but then continued checking the cell corners.

"And were you working there on the night of March 28?"

"I tried to clean up that night, but I never finished."

"And why was that?"

"Because that damned bunch of youngins had left such a mess in the basement. It looked like somebody had turned loose a pack of wild pigs in it. When kids make that kind of mess, the only thing to do is get them to clean it up. You make them clean up the first mess they make, and there won't ever be a second one to worry about."

"So you had them clean up the basement?"

"Oh no. I tried, but that bitch of a preacher's wife wouldn't allow them to dirty their hands." He shook his head in disgust. "I wouldn't be surprised if she inspected every kid's underwear before she let him go to bat on the softball field."

"You cleaned up the basement yourself then?"

"No, I threw my broom on the floor and left. For the last time, I might add. Tell me this: If the schools and churches aren't going to train young people how to act, who is?"

"What time did you leave the Tabernacle?"

"Around 8:30 or 8:45 and I came straight home. It took me about fifteen minutes."

"Could you be more exact about what time you got home?"

He ran the fingers of one hand through his short hair before answering. "It must've been just before nine because *The Real McCoys* was finishing up on television. I got myself an RC Cola and sat down to watch *The Zane Grey Theater*. When it was over, I went to bed."

"Did anyone see you between the time you left the church and the time you went to bed? Or did you talk to anyone on the phone?"

"My dog Willie came out from under the house and up on the porch when I came in, but other than him, I didn't see a soul. I couldn't talk to anybody on the phone. I've never had one in my house. If I had, the FBI would've tapped it in the last year to try to find out what rampage I was planning on the public schools."

"Mr. Eudy, I'm going to take your case, but I sure do wish you had an alibi. It is the responsibility of the prosecution to prove you're guilty, and lucky for us, they have only a handful of hard evidence. I'm sure, for example, that your fingerprints will be all over that broom, and the sheriff thinks that's what was used to strike the blows to Mrs. Gilmore's forehead that caused her to fall. As she fell, she hit the back of her skull on a cement basement step. The combined blows killed her."

"I never even thought of hitting her with my broom." He looked at me like he believed there was something wrong with my reasoning powers. "I was mad at her that night, but hell, I've been madder at students when I worked at Stanly. It wouldn't surprise me a bit if the FBI planted some of these ideas in Tubby Shepherd's head.

It would be easy to lead a sheriff in a little town to the wrong conclusions. Try investigating that possibility, Mr. Wilkie."

I got up from the wooden chair and walked to the cell door. I told him I'd get started gathering details about the case and be back to him with more questions in a few days. What I didn't tell him was that I intended to ask his brother and his neighbors about his obvious paranoia.

Chapter 9

Enough to Raise the Dead

I tried my best to get out of going to Eunice Fay Gilmore's funeral. In the first place, today was Easter Monday, and that meant no school. In the second place, I've never liked the preacher's wife. I've only gone over to the Deliverance Tabernacle for a few young people's meetings with Luke. Truth be told, the only reason I ever bothered to show up was so I could be with my boyfriend.

When Luke called me last night, he'd just come home from what he called *the viewing*. He asked me if I would go to the funeral with him today. Maybe I made a mistake long time ago not letting on that I thought Mrs. Gilmore was a nosy old biddy. Try as I might, I

101

couldn't come up with a good excuse not to go, so I ended up sitting beside him at the funeral. Turns out, I wouldn't have missed it for anything. Nothing short of *The Red Skelton Show* could top Mrs. Gilmore's sendoff at the Tabernacle.

People were stuffed into the assembly room like sardines in a tin. Luke and I had to squeeze in on a back pew beside the Peacock twins and their mama. Grady and Parks were dressed fit to kill in charcoal gray sport coats, pink button-down oxford shirts, and light gray ties. Their blonde duck-tail haircuts swirled in just the right places. I'll have to agree with what Sonny Calloway said about them the other night at the Hum Dinger. Sometimes they're more pretty than handsome. Their mama wore a black see-through blouse and a black and white pique skirt that made her look twice as fat as she really is. Big black roses are the wrong thing to put on a behind that's fifty pounds overweight.

JB Blanton led his mama in, and they settled right in front of the twins. I thought about the nasty pictures somebody had painted on the back of the choir loft. Was it JB? When Mr. White had my English class read *The Scarlet Letter*, one of his test questions asked how revenge could destroy the avenger. If JB did draw the red pictures, did he feel like he was even with her for talking to his daddy about him dating too much? Was that enough to satisfy him, or had he gone on to kill her?

Mrs. Blanton wore a giant-sized yellow straw hat that looked like something she stole off a snowman back in February. At first the Peacock boys squirmed and tried to stretch tall enough to see over the hat, but eventually they figured out they didn't have a chance. They started making jokes about it and giggling until Mrs. Blanton herself turned around and gave them a look that nailed their pretty blonde heads to the back of the pine pew. I bit my lower lip to keep from laughing out loud.

More than likely, Mrs. Gilmore's funeral drew the biggest congregation the Tabernacle will ever see. Since she'd directed the choir for years, the singers alone numbered close to fifty. They filled all the pews in the choir loft, plus half of them stood in rows on each side of the pulpit. Before they could get out the first line of "Amazing Grace," every woman up there was fumbling with Kleenexes while the men tried to carry on alone. Without the sopranos, the singing sounded so creepy it made goose bumps run up my arms. Being at the funeral of a woman somebody had murdered and stuffed into the trunk of her car didn't help me much either. But by the time the choir made it to the fourth stanza, so many were honking when they blew their noses that I had to stifle another laugh. I was relieved when they sat down and JB Blanton's daddy stood up from a front pew to make his way to the pulpit.

JB and his daddy might be junior and senior, but personally, I think it's hard to tell they're any kin. Neither one will tell you what the JB stands for, but everybody calls JB's daddy Jaybird. He's skinny and tall—mighty skinny and mighty tall—like a scarecrow put up to keep birds out of a garden. Other than Mrs. Blanton, no woman would give JB Senior a second glance. If he ever had JB's dark hair and brown eyes, you'd never know it now. A black and gray fringe of hair makes a circle around his head just above his ears. He's a farmer, so right now he's a little sunburnt from tending to his spring plants. When he stood under the bright light bulb that hung above the pulpit today, the crown of his head glowed pink. He wore a starched long-sleeved white shirt with a button-down collar but no jacket. Somebody needed to straighten his string tie for him because one end hung down way farther than the other. Too bad his wife had decided to sit at the back of the church.

JB Senior blew into the microphone a couple times and then took black-rimmed glasses from his shirt pocket and placed them on his thin nose. Even the women in the choir got hold of themselves and gave him their attention. "Friends," he began, "because we knew nobody could do it better than him, the good people of Deliverance Tabernacle of Faith gave Brother Earl Gilmore the option of preaching his own dear wife's funeral today." Jaybird turned his long, sad face and looked toward the preacher, who was sitting up front with eight or ten relatives from out of town. He then said, "He refused." Many of the church members smiled half-heartedly and nodded their heads.

Jaybird continued. "Brothers and Sisters, we Christians know that the Bible tells us to minister unto each other, so we in the church will do for Brother Gilmore today what he has so often done for us. Please listen now while members of our congregation give testimonies to the memory of Eunice Faye Gilmore. Edna Peacock will speak for the Tabernacle Church Women., and Selma Clinkscale will speak for the choir. As a deacon in this church, I will represent its officers and the congregation in general."

Rev. Gilmore sat on the front pew, as stiff as a board. His black suit and white shirt made his face look pale. When I first saw him, I thought about the husband of the deceased in some old black and white movie, not about Luke's minister or Mrs. Gilmore's husband.

When we first came into the assembly room, Luke spoke to that trampy Cecilia Shoe, who was with her preacher daddy from Charlotte. She flirted with my boyfriend like she always does. Why couldn't the Tabernacle have asked her daddy to preach at the funeral? Mrs. Gilmore never hesitated to ask Cecilia to come over and sing solos at young people's meetings. I wonder if you have to pay preachers to do funeral sermons. After I listened to Jaybird Blanton try to scrape up something good to say about Mrs. Gilmore, I decided he would have been better off paying whatever price Cecilia's daddy might've asked.

"It is my honest opinion," Jaybird said, "that Sister Gilmore always had this church's interests uppermost in her mind. Even those of us who differed with some of her ideas will admit to that fact. Many a time she made her opinion known to the church deacons through her husband, and more than a few of the changes made in this church in the past eight years are due to her suggestions."

Jaybird's speech was downright boring. I couldn't hear a soul crying now. From where I sat, it looked like Rev. Gilmore had brought his hands up and lowered his head into them. Was he crying or was he bored too?

"I know you all remember," Jaybird continued, "when we had no parking lot and had to leave our cars and trucks up and down the side of Highway 42 every Sunday. The women, especially, suffered when it rained and their high heels mired up in red mud. Sister Gilmore is the person who first came up with the plan to buy that colored feller's little farm and turn part of it into a gravel parking lot for us."

My daddy used to sell tomato plants to that old man. His name is Paul Shankle. Now that he has no farm, he's a janitor at an elementary school.

"The young people in this church owe Sister Gilmore also," Jaybird said. "I can count four or five that she has saved from the state colleges and universities by redirecting them to our denomination's Bible colleges in Bluefield, West Virginia and Garner, North Carolina."

Someone near the front said, "Amen." It was not a young person.

"This past year she was working on something else. Brother Gilmore told the deacons God had revealed to his wife that picture shows are instruments of the devil. She thought that seeing us Tabernacle folks in line to buy tickets at a box office misleads confused sinners. We could set a bad example without even knowing it, and then they might go see sinful shows that would start them on the road to Hell. She wanted us deacons to lead a campaign to boycott all picture shows."

His face looked like he'd bitten into a rotten turnip.

I've never been to a deacons' meeting at the Tabernacle, but sitting there listening to Jaybird's funeral testimony, I knew full well that he was one deacon who didn't care a whole lot for Mrs. Gilmore. The closest he came to paying her a compliment was when he told how she used to see people who were down and out and then offer them Jesus Christ as a savior. I wanted to stand up and say, "Yes, she did that for Buck Eudy and Red Byerly. Now one of them is sitting in jail accused of her murder, and Sheriff Shepherd is hunting the other one for questioning."

Jaybird had barely finished when Grady and Parks' mama put both hands on the pew in front of her and pulled her two hundred pounds up to a standing position. Why Edna Peacock hadn't sat closer to the front, I'll never know, but there she was right beside us on the second row from the back. She took time to straighten her black flowered skirt, which had ridden up on her hips. Then she noticed the top button of her fancy-collared blouse had come undone and reached to rebutton it.

JD Blanton's mama craned her neck around from the seat in front of the Peacocks to see what all the swishing and grunting was about. Somehow Mrs. Peacock's elbow jabbed Mrs. Blanton's big straw hat. The hat flew off her head and landed in the spot she had saved for Jaybird to sit after he finished his part on the program. Mrs. Peacock tried to bend over and get the hat, but bending isn't easy for a woman her size. Before she and Mrs. Blanton could recover the hat, Jaybird had made it to his family's pew. He knew there was some kind of commotion going on, but he didn't know what. He hurried to sit down.

The yellow hat crackled and crunched under Jaybird's tailbones.

"Eee, eee, eee." Parks Peacock's high-pitched giggles sounded like a chimpanzee announcing mealtime at a zoo. His brother Grady put both hands over his mouth, trying to control his snorts.

Edna Peacock decided to ignore this ruckus and get on up to the pulpit. She lifted her high-heeled left foot and stepped over Parks' creased trousers. She was a little off balance when she set her right foot down beside it, so she reached for the next twin's shoulder for support. Grady's just a mouse of a boy. I guess she startled him. Anyway, he jerked back and she grabbed his gray tie instead of his shoulder. When he tried to scoot down the pew, something like a gurgle came from his throat. He grabbed his tie and yanked. His mama's left heel sank into his ankle.

All two hundred pounds of Edna Peacock collapsed into Grady's lap. I don't think the tears running down his face had anything to do with the death of Eunice Fay Gilmore.

At this point I thought we ought to take a commercial break. That's what Red Skelton would've done.

The buzz in the congregation rose to a clamor. It was time for somebody to calm them down and get things rolling again. Jaybird Blanton would've been the one to do it, but his sunburn had deepened from pink to red while he removed two yellow hatpins from his rear end.

I was one of the few to see the undertaker start toward the front of the church. Even though he was a tall man, his arms were way too long for the rest of his body, so the sleeves of his navy blue suit left three inches of his arms hanging out. He raised his bony index finger to his lips and said, "Shh, shh" like a first grade teacher trying to quiet down children on a field trip.

Then Rev. Gilmore himself stood up, turned around, and fully faced the congregation. He announced in a stern voice, "We will skip that speaker. Get on with the final tribute." His face was as hard as one of those presidents carved on Mt. Rushmore.

The undertaker tiptoed back down the aisle. Edna Peacock got out of her son's lap and back onto the pew. A woman in the choir stood up. "That's Selma Clinkscale," Luke whispered. "She loved Sister Gilmore."

I already knew Selma Clinkscale. On weekdays she works with Mama in the draw-in room at the mill and on Sunday nights she' a carhop at the Hum Dinger. Many times when I go down to pick up my parents after work, I see her come through the gate swinging her hips and running her mouth Men look at her because she's stacked. She has full red lips and rosy cheeks, but I think those are out of a make-up box. I'll bet she dyes that orange hair of hers too.

Mama says the choir at the Tabernacle is all Selma has going for her. She didn't finish high school and she didn't get married although she's probably had lots of chances. She lives with her mama and daddy but doesn't like it. She does love to sing, though, and never misses a choir practice. Some of the choir members look down their noses at her, but the truth is she can sing a whole lot better than most of them. They tolerate her.

"I'm not good at stringing words together, so I can't give no testimony in memory of Sister Gilmore," Selma said. A twin-engine plane went by overhead. She waited till she could be heard again. Not an eye left her painted face. "I might not be able to talk but I can sing. Now I want y'all to bow your heads and I'm going to sing The Lord's Prayer. I'm doing it in memory of the woman who led this choir for seven years. Mrs. Gilmore was a woman that didn't have a whole pile of debts to ask God to forgive, but she does have a debtor now, and he might be within hearing range today. Maybe this prayer's for him too."

For a woman who claimed she couldn't talk, Selma had said right much. *Within hearing range.* She must not think Buck killed the preacher's wife. He was miles away in the county jail when she made her statement.

While she sang, I opened my eyes several times to see how people were reacting to her words. Although I was at the rear of the church and couldn't see many faces, I could see the one right beside me. Luke's eyes were wide open and he was staring right at Selma's red lips. By the time she got to *lead us not into temptation*, he was fumbling in his back pocket for his handkerchief.

Just as Selma Clinkscale was about to sit down, something thumped three times on the door at the back of the church. The

110

undertaker was standing against the door, and he almost jumped out of his skin. The door banged open and Archie Byerly stood there in a shirt and pants that were spattered with the paints he'd used on houses for who knows how many months. He stumbled halfway up the aisle.

"Where is he?" he said in a voice that carried to every pew. "Where's my boy? They said he hadda job here now. So where is he?" He held onto a pew and looked up and down the rows. Red rims circled his eyes and squiggly red roads ran through them. The undertaker recovered enough to start up the aisle behind Archie, being real slow and quiet. The congregation must've decided that it was his job, not theirs, because nobody else moved an inch.

"I say, where's he at? You know Red?" Every eye in the church was on Archie but nobody answered him. "I'm 'bout ready to go huntin' but he owes me money. You know—"

A high yelp broke in on him. Then another and another. A whole pack of yelps filled the back of the church. Fourteen mangy dogs came down the aisle with their noses to the floor tracking their master's scent. Most of them found the undertaker instead and went for his navy blue suit pants. He might know exactly what to do with dead people, but he was at a loss in the middle of those live dogs. He put his hands on his head like a migraine had suddenly hit him and rolled his eyes toward heaven. "Great God Almighty," he shouted. That just made the dogs lunge at him harder, and then he was on the floor with them. The way he waved his long arms and kicked his legs made me think of the holy rollers people say used to go to the Deliverance Tabernacle years ago.

111

Jaybird Blanton and several other men came alive and moved to help the undertaker, but Archie Byerly had beat them to it. He was not too drunk to know that his pack of hounds had caused a mess. By holding onto pews as he walked, he made it to the middle of the pack. One of the dogs was so tickled to see him that it peed on his leg.

"You stupid bitch, I'm a-gonna kill you," Archie squawked. He drew back his foot to kick the dog, but it jumped out of the way and landed in the undertaker's lap.

A gruff voice sounded from the back left corner of the church. "That's enough, that's enough." Everyone except the downed undertaker turned to see who had taken command. Red Byerly stood beside a storage closet with a large push broom in his hand. He raised it shoulder high and galloped toward the scuffling dogs. I thought he was going to brain his own father with the heavy back of the broom, but he fooled me and most of the church members too. At the last minute, he turned the brush side of his weapon downward and began sweeping the dogs down the aisle toward the door.

Rev. Gilmore left his pew at the front and took long, hard steps toward Archie Byerly and the undertaker, who had made it back to his feet. The preacher grabbed Archie's arm and looked straight into his bloodshot eyes. "This is the second time a drunken Byerly has broken into a gathering at my church," he said. "There had better not be a third."

Archie looked like he was about to answer, but the preacher gave his arm a good shake and started again. "Yes, your son does work for me now, but you are not welcome in this place. I want you to get out."

Jaybird Blanton took Archie's arm from the preacher and escorted him out of the church.

Rev. Gilmore walked to the pulpit and announced the final hymn. "We will close this service by singing Hymn 234, "When the Roll Is Called Up Yonder."

Red Skelton would have said, "Good night and God bless."

Chapter 10

Mabel's Red Pig

Mabel's Red Pig is the closest thing to a pub we have in Harmony. Not that you can get a beer there. You go to Hub's on the outskirts of town for that. What Mabel serves you is a ten-ounce glass of ice tea and a plate of the best barbecue in North Carolina. Then you pay her with two dollar bills and she hands you a quarter change. The Pig sits three buildings down from my law office. I head there for lunch on Tuesdays and Thursdays. If it were up to me, I'd go every day, but my wife likes to pack my lunch in a bag the other days. She says we need to save for my retirement. Maybe so, but I think she believes Mabel's greasy pork's going to kill me some day. There's lots worse ways to go.

When you drop by Mabel's place, you get more than just a good lunch and something to wash it down. I like talking to the men who eat there. The camaraderie is what makes this barbecue joint a little like a pub. In January, Emerson Perkins sat beside me at the Pig and told me about the fire that destroyed Belk's Bargain Basement. Emerson works in the Belks' Men's Department. He's never had a wife, so he has a barbecue plate or a barbecue sandwich at Mabel's Red Pig every day. A month later, Lonnie Furr came in from Carolina Auto Repair with a story about Lon Jr. running the shop's wrecker down an embankment and into Rhino Creek. The creek is known for the odor it carries after the mill dumps excess dye and chemicals into it. Lonnie had quite a story.

The Pig's not like the Paris bistros I drank beer in during the war, and it probably couldn't hold a candle to London's pubs. But it'll do just fine for Harmony. Yes sir, just fine.

Today I walked to the Pig for lunch, hoping Jaybird Blanton would show up for some of Mabel's barbecue like he usually does on Tuesdays. He's proud to be a deacon at the Deliverance Tabernacle, where Eunice Fay Gilmore was killed. Sometimes people who love to hear the sound of their own voices wind up saying more than they mean to. I intended to give Jaybird his chance.

When I walked in, he was sitting at the counter eating a barbecue and drinking a glass of Mabel's tea. The sleeves of his plaid work shirt showed his wrists each time he raised his glass. I sat down beside him on a chrome barstool with a little bitty red plastic seat. I don't know who those things are made for. It was hard for Jaybird to fold his long legs underneath his seat. I wouldn't be surprised if I flatten one some day when I try to balance my bulk on it. I signaled Mabel I'd have two of her barbecue sandwiches exactly like the one on Jaybird's paper plate.

"How's your Monday?" I asked him.

"Well, it's Monday, Lawyer, and one of the belts on my tractor has gone kaflooie," he answered. "But at least I got you a story today."

Jaybird attended Mrs. Gilmore's funeral yesterday. In a matter of minutes, he had me bent double laughing at his tale about Archie Byerly's pack of mongrels breaking up the affair. That story will make the rounds in Harmony for years to come.

I eased into some questions about Jaybird's church. "Can you think of any person who might have wanted Mrs. Gilmore dead?" I asked.

"Of course not."

"Had she had disagreements with church members recently? Folks in the choir she directed or young people in the church, for example."

"There's that kind of discord in all churches. I think it upset some of the sopranos when she started having Selma Clinkscale do so many solos. Before, Sister Gilmore had always taken the solo parts. When she let that good-looking, young woman step in . . . Well, you can imagine." He paused while Mabel served me my sandwiches and tea.

"You want a refill, Mr. Blanton?" she asked.

"Yes m'am," he answered. She tipped her pitcher and filled his glass.

"Can you remember any other church members she'd had trouble with?"

"It seems like she was mighty sour on the men in our church these last months. I got no idea why. She even made my boy JB mad several weeks back. Came to me saying it was unwise to allow him to date so many different girls and go off places with them more often than he came to church. I cut back on his dates."

"Uh huh," I said between bites of barbecue.

"He's still mad at her, but he'll get over it."

"Was there anything else to indicate she'd lost respect for men?"

"Oh yes. It was hard not to notice. Every month that went by, she got rougher on the men in our congregation. Back in February, the Men's Council decided we'd have us a fish fry this summer—not invite the families though, just the Men's Fellowship. Hubie Fort can fry fish with the best of them. He said he'd head up the cooking. We had a lot of planning left to do, but it never got done."

I smiled at Jaybird's mention of Hubie Fort, who lives in one bedroom of his brother's house. I think he cooks and cleans for his brother's wife. Hubie stands about five feet tall and might weigh a hundred thirty pounds in December when he's bundled up in a wool sweater and heavy shoes. His head is small, bald, and shiny. It was that way the first time I remember seeing him around Harmony and that was twenty-five years ago. He's in his sixties now but has never been married. His voice is soft and sweet, almost like a purr. I bet he sings in the Tabernacle's choir.

"I would've thought any idea that included Hubie would appeal to your preacher," I said. "A few years back word about town had it that Rev. Gilmore's sermons were the main reason Hubie left his church and went way out there to the Tabernacle. The Forts have always been Presbyterians. It was a blow to the family pride when Hubie moved to a Pentecostal church." I was careful not to say *holy roller*.

Jaybird raised his eyebrows briefly and said, "I guess Brother Gilmore took the fish fry idea home to his wife. Anyway, she made a point of singling out each man on the Council and letting him know in no uncertain terms that God's house was no place for a fish fry, not even if we had it in the basement. When it got to be my time to listen to her sermon, I asked her if she didn't remember reading in the Scriptures about Jesus giving a little fish fry of his own. She looked at me like I'd sprouted horns and a tail. Then she said the Savior had never done any such thing. I screwed up my courage and mentioned Him feeding the five thousand with five loaves and two fishes. I went on to tell her I bet those fishes had been fried."

Jaybird's face broke into a wide grin. I slapped my hand on my hip and laughed out loud.

"According to her, that was entirely different because it was a miracle Jesus had put to a special use. She said what the Council was suggesting was more like something some church in Black Bottom might do on a Saturday night."

"So what's wrong with a fish fry at a colored church?" I said. "Lots of praying and singing are done at them. She ought to approve of that."

"Testifying too. But she claimed she'd have thought white men would know better."

"That so?"

"Said we'd start out having fish fries, and the next thing you knew, we'd be bringing liquor and women to them. I don't know where she came up with that one. To me it seemed like she was being way too suspicious. After all, every one of us in the Men's Fellowship is a Christian. Anyway, I decided not to tangle with her anymore. The Council dropped the fish fry."

Jaybird rubbed his chin and thought for a moment or two. "I told you, Lawyer Wilkie," he said, "that kind of discord is common in churches. Don't get the notion there's a murderer sitting in our congregation because there ain't."

"I understand. But I know Buck Eudy's sitting in the county jail, and I'm fairly sure he's not a murderer either. Can you bear with me for a couple more questions?"

"Shore."

"Did anybody ever tell Rev. Gilmore what Mrs. Gilmore said about the plans for the fish fry?"

119

"We tried to but it was like he didn't want to hear it. I think he was afraid of her sometimes." He took a long swallow of his tea and then bent his head closer to mine and lowered his voice. "My wife said it was the Change of Life making her so cranky," he said. "Myself, I say it was a streak of pure meanness."

Some years ago, Maizie went through her own share of hot flashes and mood swings. Jaybird's assessment of Mrs. Gilmore's problem made me smile before I continued my questions. "Did the preacher and his wife have a good marriage?" I asked.

"Far as I know."

"Were they affectionate toward each other?"

"Lawyer, you need to understand something. Sister Gilmore tried to keep our young people straight. She wanted them coming to church instead of going off to places like movies, where they might yield to temptation. You get my point?"

"Yes."

"So, it stands to reason she and the preacher ain't going to be hugging and kissing each other at the church. Now, in their own home—I can't say about that."

"You've never heard of any problems they had?"

"Oh, some years back—maybe around 1952 or 53—a rumor circulated. I think somebody in the choir saw Brother Gilmore with his arm around a woman he was counseling. Her husband had run off and left her and a youngin' or two."

"Hmm," I said. "But you've never seen him put his arm around his wife—not at the church?" Jaybird might have answered if

Mabel hadn't appeared again to refill our tea glasses. By the time she finished, he had some questions of his own.

"Listen here, Lawyer," he said. "Up until Thursday night, the man you've decided to defend worked at my church. Why don't you ask me some questions about him? If you're digging up people's pasts, start digging in Buck Eudy's backyard. See what you can find about his temper. The night of the softball cookout that man lost his temper one time too many and killed Sister Gilmore."

I had more questions for Jaybird—some about Buck and some about Red Byerly—but our discussion had become too heated. They would have to wait for another lunch at the Pig. "I'm sorry you feel that way," I said. "My client does have difficulty controlling his temper. A year ago, he paid for his problem with his job. Last Friday night in your church, he used inappropriate language, threw down a push broom, and spit on the basement floor. I hope to prove he did not kill Eunice Gilmore. His temper cost him his job again, but he shouldn't have to pay with his life."

Jaybird spun his little barstool around. His elbow bumped his half-empty glass, and tea spread across the counter. As he strode toward the door, he turned his head and said, "Maybe you'd be better off sticking to your wills and tax forms, Lawyer."

Chapter 11

A Learning Experience

It's hard for me to understand why people complain so about having to go back to school after a holiday. When Mama went to work on Easter Monday and we still had another day of vacation, she left a list for us girls:

> Defrost Frigidaire.
> Clean stove. Line burners with tin foil.
> Straighten out your closet.
> Clean bathroom.

She knew I had to go to the funeral with Luke, but she made her little list anyway. A grimy kitchen, a crammed closet, a stinking toilet bowl—put these up against Mr. White's English class or Miss Stewart's psychology class. You'd have to be stupid to want to stay home rather than go on back to school.

Harmony High has only one psych class, and Miss Stewart interviews every kid who wants to be part of it. Only five juniors made the class this year. I was one of the lucky ones. Our teacher loves to have us do experiments and projects, so it came as no surprise when she assigned a learning project Tuesday morning after Easter. She wants us to spend four weeks learning how to do something we've never done before. We have to keep notes on each learning session and make charts of our progress, including plateaus we reach. In class we spent a half hour talking about what we might choose to learn. A lot of people jumped in when Miss Stewart mentioned playing musical instruments. Catherine Love said she's going to learn to play her mother's flute if she can find it in their attic. Frank Bello wants to have a go at his Italian uncle's violin. Three girls decided to learn to play the piano.

Playing a musical instrument is the last thing in the world I'd try to learn. When I was twelve years old, I convinced my mama my heart would never be happy until I owned a piano and learned to play it. Mama had nothing when she was growing up. There was no radio in her house, much less a piano. So she wants Linda Sue and me to have things she didn't. She bought me a second-hand upright piano and found a two-hundred-and-fifty-year-old lady with blue hair to

123

give me a lesson every week. For a whole year I went to that woman's house and banged the keys of her baby-grand. More often than not when I sat down at her Steinway on Saturday, I had not touched the keys of my Kimball to practice all week. We sold it a year later and it shouldn't have been called *third hand.*

When the people in psychology class discussed what they might do, the first thing that came to my mind was learning to crochet. In our house we have one crocheted piece that my mama's mama made. I guess you'd call it a blanket. It may have started out white, but it's almost yellow now. Mama says it kept her warm when she weighed less than a tabby cat and slept in the top drawer of a chest of drawers. I sat there thinking about how Mama would drape whatever I crocheted over the back of her oak rocker like she's done Grandma's piece.

But then that sissified Ray Phillips announced to the class what he plans to do for his project. He thinks he'll learn to cross stitch, whatever that is, and will do something with a beehive and bees like his grandmother did years ago.

His idea reminded me of mine, except it was better, much better. I gritted my teeth because my daddy keeps bees. Why hadn't I come up with a bee project? Maybe I could get Daddy to teach me to be a beekeeper. No, that would never do. He says a bee can tell when you're afraid of it and will sting you in spite of all you do. I don't have any trouble squatting and watching one work over a clover blossom, but it's beyond me how Daddy sticks his hand into the home of a million bees and steals a rack of their honey.

The bees got my mind going about Daddy. Linda Sue is my mama's girl and I am my daddy's. Neither one of them would ever admit that, but it's the truth anyway. It doesn't bother me at all, Linda Sue neither. We think it's fair. Each one of us is a favorite. Linda Sue will mess around for hours in the kitchen with Mama making banana pudding or coconut cake. The two of them watch *The Ed Sullivan Show* sitting on the couch embroidering twin pillow cases. Me—I'd rather help Daddy paint the back porch steps or build bluebird houses.

While my classmates went on and on about what they planned to learn, I tried to figure out some project Daddy and I could work on together. I remembered hearing a story about him and Uncle Curly treeing a coon one night. Daddy spotted the coon first, so it should've been his. He saw how easy it was going to be to shoot it though, and he decided to let his younger brother have it. While Uncle Curly was taking aim, Daddy leaned his gun up against the tree and walked out into the bushes to relieve himself. Lo and behold (Daddy likes to say that when he's coming up on the good part of this story), if Daddy didn't roust out a skunk that was hiding in the very bushes he was peeing in. The critter didn't like his shower bath and sprayed Daddy full force. Daddy let out a yell. Uncle Curly misfired and then stumbled over Daddy's gun. It went off and the coon fell from the tree limb dead.

Uncle Curly claims to have killed the coon, but Daddy says the coon died of the skunk's odor. Mama wouldn't let him sleep in the bed with her that night and says it was mighty hard to have any appetite sitting at the breakfast table with him next day.

125

All that went on before I was born. When Linda Sue and I came along, Mama made Daddy sell his gun to some man down at the mill. I don't think Uncle Curly hunts any more either, but both of them like to go fishing once in a while. Daddy taught me to fish in the ocean when I was barely ten years old, but I totally missed out on the hunting.

My mind was made up. I'd learn to shoot a gun.

That evening I took the idea home with me and brought it up at supper when Mama asked what we'd done in school that day. First, I told them the details of Miss Stewart's project. Mama and Daddy both thought it sounded fine, but any idea that came out of Miss Belle Stewart's head would have sounded good to them. She's the only teacher who's paid an official visit to our house since I've been in high school. She didn't just sit in the living room talking to Mama about psychology that day either. When she found out Daddy was in his garden gathering turnips for supper, she went down there and talked to him too. Later his voice sounded proud when he told us how she tried to buy a mess of turnips from him and how she helped him pull the ones he gave her. Since they liked Miss Stewart and her learning project, I hoped they would agree with the shooting idea I'd come up with.

"What I want to do is learn to shoot a rifle," I began. "You could teach me three days a week after you come home from work, Daddy." I stared straight at him, but I could see Mama's face out of the corner of my eye. She looked like I had said I was thinking of learning to skin cats and was going to use a neighbor's kitten as my first victim.

"Guns are dangerous, Jonnie." She hadn't given Daddy a chance to answer me. "Besides, you'd never use what you learn. Why don't you learn to make biscuits? I'd be glad to teach you, and it would help me out cooking supper too."

I'd let my eyes leave Daddy's face for only a couple seconds while she talked and instead of answering her, I sent him an ESP message. *Help me, Daddy. Help me.*

Linda Sue started to put in her two cents worth, which nobody had asked for, but Daddy spoke up. "Lois, if I did the teaching and I watched everything she did close, we could take a lot of the danger out."

"John, you don't even have a rifle." Mama sounded irritated.

"No, but I think Curly still has his twenty-two. I'll call him up and find out." I could tell Daddy wanted to teach me to shoot and I knew Mama would give in. She'd worry every day we went out to practice and complain about us giving her more gray hairs, but she'd let Daddy teach me to use a rifle because she could see how bad he wanted to do it.

I was right. By Thursday afternoon, Daddy and I had cleaned Uncle Curly's rifle, bought ammunition for it, bought three targets, and found a place for my lessons. Fifty yards behind our house, a steep bank drops to the railroad tracks. On our side of the tracks is Daddy's garden. On the other side are heavy woods. Our land lies inside the city limits where shooting is against the law, but Buck's land is the first piece outside the city limits and hunting is legal there. A short walk down the tracks would get Daddy and me to a legal shooting spot.

Years ago when their money was real tight, Daddy made a path from the garden down to the railroad. During the Great Depression he and Mama walked down the tracks to and from work every day. They saved gas and it was shorter than walking on the street because the railroad tracks were laid straight to the mill where men loaded cloth into the boxcars to be shipped all over the country. Mama and Daddy have told us girls over and over to stay away from the path and the tracks. Not only are the trains dangerous, but also people have been known to use the woods across the tracks for drinking parties on weekends.

After supper Daddy and I made our way through the brambles down the steep path. Following behind Daddy, I stared at the rifle he carried and felt like I was Nancy Drew walking into *Mystery down the Railroad Bank*. But shoot, hadn't Mrs. Gilmore's death put me in the middle of a real mystery? At the bottom of the path, Daddy stopped to get his breath, and I picked a cocklebur off one of my socks. I saw a little smear of blood just above it on my leg.

"Next time, wear you some long socks," Daddy said. "And keep your eyes open for poison ivy. It might be a little early for it, but you don't want to give your mama another reason to find you a cooking project."

I laughed.

"I figure we better walk down the tracks a ways till we get outside the city limits and out of hearing range of the house," he said. "You know your mama's as jumpy as a cat, and if she hears our rifle shots, she'll be nervous the whole time we're down here."

We walked along beside the tracks. Granite gravel the size of fifty-cent pieces lay up close to them. Some had scattered into the brown grass where we were walking. Almost nobody walks these tracks any more. Maybe a few little boys ignore their parents' warnings and came down here exploring once in a while. That's about all.

It popped into my mind that Red Byerly's mama had died somewhere in the woods on the other side of the tracks. "Didn't Rose Byerly get killed down here, Daddy?" I asked.

He hesitated a minute. "No," he finally answered. "That was about a mile past the mill and in the woods near Black Bottom. It musta been five or six years ago now. Never did find out who killed her."

"What would a white woman be doing there?" I asked.

"Watch out for this big rock," he said. He didn't slow down or take his eyes off the ground.

A nice little colored community named Elmira lies about a half mile from the other side of the tracks. "You reckon a colored man killed her?" I asked and then held my breath.

"I don't know who was down there with her. Nobody does. But anybody out in them woods after midnight is up to no good" he said.

129

"But do you think it was a colored man?" I asked

"It coulda been, but not necessarily. Spencer is just up the road apiece, maybe twelve miles west of here. It's a railroad hub of sorts. Lots of the railroad men sleep there overnight before they take on another train. Word has it that some of them used to come back here—" He broke off but I waited for him to finish.

"Jonnie, that's something you can ask your mama about. Or better yet, just let it go."

I knew not to look up at him. Mama had told Linda Sue and me about menstruation and where babies come from, but until that moment, my daddy had never come close to talking about sex in front of me. I suddenly felt older.

"So you think a railroad man could've done it," I said.

"I didn't say that. They weren't the only ones that came down here. At the mill on Monday mornings, you'd hear about drinking that went on across the tracks on Saturday nights. During the Depression I kept meat in our frying pan by setting rabbit boxes over yonder in the woods. Many's the time I found dead camp fires with liquor bottles around them. Other things too."

"Was Rose Byerly shot?" I asked.

"That's right," he said, "and she was half neked too."

"I don't understand why they didn't find her killer. Was it a big thing in the paper like Mrs. Gilmore's story is?"

"Oh, it made the paper all right. I believe it stayed there for several days. But it was nothing like Mrs. Gilmore, nothing at all. People in Harmony expected such things out of the likes of Rose

Byerly, but Mrs. Gilmore was a preacher's wife. From what I hear, she was a lot like a preacher herself. It's news when somebody like her is killed, and everybody wants to have the killer brought to justice."

"I guess you're right but both of them were God's children," I answered.

"Yes, but let me give you another example. Say Mr. Davidson's brand new Cadillac was to be stole out of the mill's parking lot while he was in his office one day. It would make the paper for days, and the police wouldn't be satisfied until they found it and got it back to him. Not only that, but they'd throw the man who stole it in jail. And that's as it should be, ain't it?"

Sometimes Daddy acts like he thinks the man who owns Harmony Mills is a good king and Harmony is his little country.

"Oh yes," I replied.

"But now, if somebody stole a beat-up 46 Ford from some feller over in Black Bottom who hadn't struck a lick to support hisself in twenty years, what would you think if *The Telegram* run stories about it day after day and the Harmony police force did nothing else till they found that car and the man who took it?"

I decided it would be better to just drop the subject. When Daddy gets a notion in his head, it can be hard to straighten him out. Besides, I knew better than to cross him at the beginning of this four-week learning project. I sure would've liked to ask more about Rose Byerly, but he stopped beside the track, ready to start my lesson.

I followed his directions and took ten bullets out of the blue and red carton he'd had me carry. They were smaller than I had pictured them, less than an inch long. I ran my fingers over one. The sides were smooth and cold. The back part was a dull gold color and the front tip was a dead gray. *Bullets.* The ugly name fit

I handed the bullets to Daddy. "Watch how I load this thing," he said. One by one he fed five into the black hole. "Guns can kill," he said, "but only when one of us pulls the trigger." He lifted his eyes to my face and added, "It's enough to keep you sober."

I gave a half-laugh. "And enough to keep me shooting at paper targets," I said.

He passed me the rifle and the last five bullets. "Okay, it's your turn," he said. "Do it just like I did." It took me twice as long as it had him. I was glad when the last bullet slid into its place.

He nodded once and said, "That's good. You not nervous, are you?"

"No." It was a lie and he knew it was a lie.

"This last part's as important as anything I've taught you so far," he said. "Maybe more-so." He pointed at a little grey metal thing on top the rifle. "This here's the safety and you want to always keep it on except when you're actually ready to fire." He clicked it off and then on again.

"Now put the gun down on that flat place and gimmie one of the targets you picked out at the hardware store," Daddy said. "You stay here while I find a tree to hang it on." I watched him walk what I thought was way too far down the tracks before he crossed over the rails, took his hammer and a nail out of his back overall pocket, and tacked the white square to a big pine tree. I wished there was a tree on our side of the tracks big enough to hold the target, but our side was overgrown with weeds and briars.

I studied the black crossties that stretched out for sixty or seventy yards in front of me and then curved to the right around the railroad bank and disappeared. I wondered what might be around that bend and then I smiled to myself. I have to admit I'm not much different from the little boys who disobey their mamas and daddies to come exploring down here.

Daddy made his way back up the tracks and picked up the rifle. He then explained one more time how careful you have to be when you handle a gun. Finally, he demonstrated how I should stand, hold the rifle, release the safety, pull back the bolt, take aim, and squeeze the trigger. Then he closed one eye, aimed, and fired. The bullet casing flew off to the side and hit the rocks by the tracks. To my surprise, his very first shot hit the target. I couldn't see well enough to tell if it was a bull's-eye but it sure was a square hit. So were his next two.

He handed me the rifle and I was careful to do exactly like he'd told me. When I lined up the target in the site though, I froze.

"Something's moving down there," I said.

"Lower your gun and put on the safety, Jonnie." There was a frown in his voice.

"Do you see it?" I asked.

"Yeah. Lay the gun on the ground." He craned his neck and stared down the track. "Now, you just stay put. I'm going down there and see what it is."

I would have given half the money in my dime bank to go with him, but he was gone before I could argue with him.

It didn't take him nearly as long to get to the big pine tree this time as it had when he'd gone to put up the target. He walked several yards beyond it and disappeared in some scrub oaks. I counted to two hundred but still saw no sign of him. At four hundred, he came out of the oaks and jerked the target off the pine tree. My heart sank.

What had he found down there? A hundred things ran through my mind. Just as Daddy stepped away from the pine and started to recross the tracks, a heavy-set colored man stuck his head out through the scrub oaks. He lumbered like Alley Oop toward the tracks. It was no time before he stumbled and fell to his knees. Daddy heard him and turned around. He pointed his finger at the man and said in a loud voice, "You better sober up like I told you. The trains that run on these tracks can kill you as easy as a rifle can."

I looked down at the rifle lying beside me in the brown grass and then back down the tracks at the colored man.

Daddy pointed to a spot behind the pine and shouted, "Go over there and sit on that rock until I can climb back up the railroad bank." His voice dropped back to normal, but I thought I heard him tell the colored man something or other about Mama.

He turned and made his way back down the tracks toward me. I realized my heart was going way too fast. Daddy and I had aimed the rifle pretty close to where the man's head had popped up. Daddy had shot that gun as true as Marshall Dillon on *Gunsmoke*, and thank heavens I'd never pulled the trigger.

He was halfway back to me when I heard a train in the distance. I moved away from the tracks and watched the drunk man stumble back into the scrub oaks. Behind Daddy, the train engine came around the curve and into sight. It roared louder and louder, and I moved back from the tracks another yard. The engineer saw Daddy and maybe me too. He sounded his whistle twice. I imagined the nervous jitter it'd sent through Mama back in the house.

Daddy reached me and his arm went round my shoulder just as the engine passed. We stood and listened to the clack, clack, clack of wheels meeting rails while boxcar after boxcar rolled past us.

As the noise moved on down the tracks, I could hardly wait to hear the story I knew my daddy was going to tell. "What in the world was that man doing behind our target?" I asked.

Daddy's face was serious. "He wasn't behind it until I put it up," he said. "You might say we moved into his territory where he wasn't bothering a soul."

"Was he drunk?" I asked.

"High as a kite," Daddy answered and squeezed his lips together trying to keep a grin from spreading across his face. "He said he lives a mile or so back that way." He pointed across the tracks toward Elmira.

"He came close to living nowhere. What if I hadn't seen him moving around?"

135

"Seems like he had a spat with his girlfriend last night and he's been drinking ever since. He'd passed out on a big rock back behind where I nailed the target. When I fired them shots, he thought he was a goner."

"Why did you tell him you had to talk to Mama?" I asked.

"We had one hot dog and some corn left after supper. I thought that and maybe a Mason jar of strong coffee might get him back on the right track," he said.

"That's like when Mama used to feed hobos on the back steps during the Depression," I said. I'd heard her talk about giving plates of vegetables to men who climbed up the railroad bank and knocked on our back door.

"A little bit, yes. But I think you and me owe this man something. What you think?"

"We do." I nodded.

He bent to pick up the rifle. "And Jonnie," he said, "maybe you ought to reconsider your learning project. Ain't nothing better than a pan of your mama's biscuits when we sit down to supper. Learning to make them the way she does wouldn't be a waste of your time. I want you to think about it."

"I don't have to think about it." I said as he straightened up and took the remaining bullets out of the rifle. "You'll get to try my first batch tomorrow at supper."

Chapter 12

House Calls

A few of Harmony's doctors still make house calls when somebody's deathly ill, but they do it grudgingly. We lawyers have even less reason to travel to private homes than do our doctor friends. This afternoon as I drove to West Harmony seeking information about Buck Eudy, I felt more like a private detective than a lawyer. I can't say I minded the experience. It beat sitting in my office finishing up the tax forms mill folks have been bringing in since early March.

Clyde and Beedie Cooley own the small frame house on one side of the Eudy property. Both are deaf mutes. I knew that before I bruised my knuckles beating on their front door. Having failed to rouse them there, I moved toward the back door. I peeped into every window as I made my way through the pansies that border the entire east side of their house. Near the rear I put my face up against what I guessed was a kitchen window about five feet above the ground. A pale wrinkled face framed with white hair appeared just as I was about to begin pounding on the glass. Both of our mouths flew open. If Mrs. Cooley hadn't been mute, I suppose she would've screamed. I came close to it myself.

She disappeared for a minute, and I had my business card pressed to the window when her husband's equally wrinkled face filled the place she'd vacated. Eventually, I was allowed to enter their house and sit in their tiny Victorian parlor. We scribbled notes on a tablet that looked like the ones used by children in grammar schools. They've known Buck since he was a little boy and can't believe he would harm anyone. He brings them a fruit cake every Christmas. Last year he repaired their grandfather clock and refused to take a penny's pay. They have no TV, thus were in bed asleep at the time Buck said he returned from the Deliverance Tabernacle last Thursday night. I found the Cooleys charming but they were of little help.

I left their cottage and looked across the street at a little frame house. The blinds were drawn and the grass needed cutting. My friend Tubby Shepherd had informed me I would find no one home there. Wesley Clinton, a bachelor, rents it but is seldom home. He works as a traveling salesman selling Raleigh Home Products from North Carolina down through Georgia. After talking to the young man's parents and his boss, Tubby caught up with him by phone in Rock

Hill, South Carolina. He learned that Clinton has been out on his current trip for ten days and won't return home for another four.

I made a right turn into John and Lois Sparks' driveway. Their neat white frame house with blue roof and black shutters is larger than most on the street. I'd guess it has five rooms. A small wooden sign with *Harmony* printed in black letters stands by the street between their property and Buck's. They're inside and he's outside the city limits. Many of the houses on that end of Gibson Street were built or purchased by mill workers who worked long and hard to get out of the three-room rent houses C. B. Davidson built near Plant 6 for his employees twenty-five years ago. John Sparks' driveway is gravel but a new cement sidewalk leads to his front porch. He and Lois have planted boxwoods all along the walk, and the red azaleas up close to the house put to shame the ones Maizie bought at Harmony Nursery last week.

The daughter who answered the doorbell looked like something you might see on a magazine cover. Black hair and blue eyes make for an unusual combination. I thought how proud the Sparks must be of this girl. Almost immediately, Lois entered with a second daughter, a little blonde, and I knew they had another reason to be proud.

When John came in, he and Lois sat down with me, and then Lois instructed the girls to finish cooking the supper she'd started. Folks up on that end of town eat earlier than folks down on my end.

George Eudy had told me that the Sparks family hadn't heard his brother return home after work on the night of the murder. John confirmed this fact, and his younger daughter stuck her head back into the living room to announce that she and her sister almost never hear Buck's truck at night unless their bedroom windows are open.

Her mother turned toward the door and said, "Cut the burners down to simmer, Linda Sue. You and Jonnie might as well come on back in here." To me, she said, "I know how curious my girls are. Besides, they might remember something John and I don't. They're real worried about Buck."

The older girl sat beside me on the sofa. The little sister chose the front edge of the ottoman near her mother's chair. I asked the family if they had noticed any unusual behavior on Buck's part in the past six months. Lois gave John a quick look. Both girls' eyes got wide. I sat and waited.

Worry lines appeared on Lois's forehead, and she stared at me as if I had asked a confusing question. "Well, Lawyer Wilkie," she said, "Buck has been peculiar all his life."

I tried again. "Can you think of anything you've seen him do recently that was out of the ordinary, something that surprised or shocked you?"

Lois and John swapped a long look. I could almost hear them making a joint decision. John folded his arms across his chest and then put his right hand on his chin just under his mouth. He moved his head from side to side like the words he was about to speak were already bothering him. "There was a Saturday back in February that made me wonder if Buck was losing his mind," he finally said.

Lois looked down into her lap.

The girls still sat wide eyed.

"When I talked to Buck in the county jail last Monday," I said, "his comments made me think he might have some sort of mental disorder. I spoke with old Doc Boger, whom the Eudys depended on up until he retired. He said Sergeant Eudy suffered mental problems during the 1940's. That was Buck's uncle."

John's eyes lit up. "That's right," he said. "Everybody around here knows his story. His trouble started when he backed his car over his wife's daddy. Killed him."

One of the girls gasped.

"He didn't mean to," Lois added quickly. "The old man was up under the car trying to change the oil, and Sarge didn't know he was there."

"Sarge never got over it," John said. "And he never drove a car again. People would see him walking all over creation. Sometimes in the dead of night. His neighbors complained about him sitting naked on his front porch when the summer temperatures got high."

"John," Lois said, cutting her eyes from her husband's face to each of her girls.

"Where did he live?" I asked.

"About six houses past Commodore and Miss Lillie," Lois answered. "He built that stone house with the big chimney in front as a wedding present for his wife. We always thought it looked out of place here on Gibson Street. A Greek couple with three children lives in it now. They bought it when Sarge died and his wife moved in with her brother and his family." At the end of that sentence, Lois pushed her glasses up off her nose and paused a few seconds.

"You know her brother served as a senator down in Raleigh for years, don't you?" she continued in a confidential tone.

"Yes, I've heard that."

"People say that's why Sarge was never sent away to Morganton. His wife had connections."

I decided not to touch that one. "Well, it appears Buck isn't the first Eudy to suffer mental problems," I said. "John, you started to tell me about an unusual incident, didn't you?"

John wrinkled his brow and thought a minute. "I was cutting back my wisteria vine that morning like I do every February. My back was to the street, but when I needed to move my ladder, I saw something out of the corner of my eye. Something that didn't belong. I walked toward the street and Buck was up there in the ditch crawling on his belly. Looked like something you might see in a war movie. You know, like soldiers in the trenches."

I nodded.

"When I got up close enough, I asked him what he was doing in the ditch. He commenced to tell me he'd seen FBI men talking to me that morning." John rolled his eyes. "I knew full well who he meant. Two Jehovah's Witnesses had wasted my time trying to give me copies of *The Watchtower* thirty minutes before. To my mind they hadn't looked as suspicious standing there in their black pants and white shirts as Buck did crawling around on his belly in his overalls."

I smiled. John Sparks is a good storyteller.

"Lois saw us from the window and knew something was bad wrong," he continued. She came out to the street, and we helped Buck up off the ground and got him into the house where he could get warm. This was February but he didn't even have on a coat. Lois made a pot of hot coffee." He pointed toward the kitchen. "The three of us sat in there at the table and drank it."

I had been taking notes on a legal pad but stopped to ask if they were able to convince Buck the men were Jehovah's Witnesses. They said they'd tried but to no avail.

Lois took up the story. "While we were sitting around the table, Buck's eyes looked like an animal's some hunter had cornered with a gun. He asked me if I ever saw men coming up the railroad bank and across our garden. I told him the only people who'd done that since the Depression ended twenty years ago were little colored boys from across the tracks trying to steal them a watermelon out of John's garden. But Buck claimed to have seen men dressed in camouflage suits tramping around between his house and the railroad tracks. He thought part of them traveled in a helicopter and they all talked to each other on walkie talkies."

Linda Sue giggled, but her mama's sharp look told her this was no time for laughing.

Lois continued. "He finished his coffee, and just before he got up to go, he said, 'You and your girls don't need to worry about them, Lois. It's me they're after, not you. They think if they get enough lies on me, they can land me in jail.'"

Her voice got lower and she looked back down at her lap. "And jail is where he is right now," she said.

I told Lois I thought Buck was innocent of the murder charge and would come out of that jail a free man. I could tell she wanted to believe me, but she didn't smile.

Turning to the girls, I asked if they had noted unusual behavior in their neighbor. Jonnie spoke right up.

"I see him out in the back feeding his dog lots of times. He throws up his hand or says hey to me. Nothing strange."

The younger sister squirmed and wrinkled her brow. There was no doubt in my mind that she knew something more. "If you don't tell, I'm going to," she said to her sister.

Lois smiled over at Jonnie and then looked at me. "Jonnie likes Buck a whole lot," she said. "He's helped her understand school work that had her baffled. Of course, it was way over mine and John's heads too." Then she turned to her daughter. "Remember that Lawyer Wilkie is on Buck's side, Jonnie," she said. "It's okay to tell him whatever you know."

Jonnie looked at her little sister like she wanted to launch her into orbit, but then she turned and said to me, "This has nothing to do with Mrs. Gilmore's death but here it is, for whatever it's worth. One afternoon last summer before Mama and Daddy came home from work, Buck was working with a swing blade clearing the back edge of his lot next to Daddy's beehives."

A train whistle sounded in the distance, making me realize just how close the Sparks home was to the railroad tracks.

144

Jonnie continued. "He saw Linda Sue and me on our way down to the garden to pick some tomatoes and cucumbers for supper, and he stopped his work and motioned for us to wait a minute." The rumble of the freight train almost drowned out her last words. She paused until it was past.

"We met him at the beehives, and he asked us if we ever noticed funny noises coming out of them. Of course, we told him no."

Her sister broke in. "Then he walked right up to the first hive and bent down so his ear wasn't six inches from that little slit where the bees go in and out. I don't know about Jonnie," she said looking at her sister, "but as far as I'm concerned, you couldn't *pay* me to put my ear down to that slit."

"Linda Sue," Jonnie said, "I was in the middle of my story." She looked back over at me. "We told Buck Daddy's bees were just going about the business of making honey the way they always do. He said to let him know if Daddy ever found any radio equipment planted in the honey racks."

"And Jonnie told me there was no reason to bother Daddy with the story, that Buck was a little bit addled." Linda Sue looked at her daddy and shrugged her shoulders as if to say she hadn't understood her sister's decision. "So we didn't," she said and smirked at Jonnie.

That spunky little girl reminded me of myself as a kid. My brother was two years older than me, and nothing made me happier than informing our parents when he'd made a mistake. Unfortunately, the favor I now planned to ask of Jonnie would burst the balloon Linda Sue had just blown up for herself.

Chapter 13

Bloodhounds

Lawyer Clayton Wilkie showed up at our house this evening right after Mama and Daddy got home from the mill. I'd heard them talk about him before, but up until I answered the front door, I'd never had any reason to imagine what he looked like. While he was telling me who he was, Mama came out of the kitchen wiping her wet hands on a dish towel. When he turned his head quickly to say hello to her, his jowls flopped like a bloodhound's.

Linda Sue came in and Mama introduced us and asked him to sit down there in the living room, which is a place saved for special company and my dates. Before he reached the couch, he took a white handkerchief out of his back pocket and wiped the sweat off his bald head and forehead. April seldom makes folks around here sweat, but I guess people his size do it year round.

None of us minded talking to the lawyer until he started asking about Buck's behavior. George Eudy hadn't asked about it, so we hadn't volunteered to tell him about the FBI men or any of that stuff. I don't think we wanted to gossip about something that would make Buck look like a fool to his older brother. Lawyer Wilkie made us realize he was going to do his best to help Buck, though, so we went ahead and opened up.

He took notes on top of notes while we talked. Afterward, he ran his finger down several of the pages, and then said, "I'm not a psychiatrist but it seems like Buck's got a case of paranoia." He explained what that is, and I smiled because Miss Stewart talked about paranoia for an entire class period back in the winter. Then the lawyer put both his big hands behind the folds of his neck and thought for a minute. "If Buck could afford all three, his case needs a psychiatrist, a private detective, and me," he said. "As it is, he only has me."

He had left us with nothing to say, so he went on. "Somebody knows more than they're telling." He turned his face toward me. "Jonnie, I haven't learned much from the young people who were present at the softball cookout the night of Mrs. Gilmore's death. One of them did mention that you sometimes visit youth programs at their church. He thought I might want to question you since you live beside Buck."

148

"Another softball sleuth," said Linda Sue. It was killing her for me to get all this attention.

"I wonder if you could keep your ears to the ground for information about Red Byerly, the softball team, or anything else that might shed some light on Buck's case." He raised his droopy eyelids and waited.

It was his *anything else* that bothered me. Nasty pictures of Mrs. Gilmore painted on a back wall of the Deliverance Tabernacle fit into the *anything else* category. I knew they might lead to a suspect other than Buck, but I'd promised Luke I'd keep my mouth shut about them. He'd said, the preacher or some of the deacons would have mentioned them to Tubby Shepherd. I hoped he was right.

I put my better judgment on a back burner and pictured myself with my nose to the ground. I saw a bloodhound with ears as floppy as the lawyer's jaws. "Oh, I'll be glad to do some snooping for you," I said. "I have a date with one of the softball players tomorrow night."

"For that matter, it's every Saturday night," Linda Sue popped in. Nobody paid her any mind.

"I wish you would make notes on things that come up and mail them to me or drop then at my office on Church Street." He fiddled in his shirt pocket and brought out two business cards. He handed one to Daddy and one to me. I don't know about Daddy, but I felt ten feet tall.

Daddy saw Lawyer Wilkie out the front door and Mama told us girls to come help her finish supper. "Jonnie, get the flour and buttermilk," she said. "You're going to get to make those biscuits, after all." She bent down to take the Jewel lard and the wooden mixing bowl from the cabinet. I got the buttermilk out of the Frigidaire, but I wondered how my mama could be so interested in biscuits when the lawyer had just asked me to be his partner.

We worked side by side at the counter top. She poured flour, salt, and baking powder into the sifter for me and then reached up to wipe a tear out of the corner of her right eye. She shook her head back and forth real slow like she'd just lost hope of ever making another good biscuit.

I poured in the buttermilk she'd measured out for me. "What's wrong, Mama?" I asked. My voice was quiet. I hadn't seen her cry more than a half dozen times in my life.

"Go ahead and mix that up and then start kneading the dough," she said. She crossed the kitchen to pull a Kleenex out of the box on top of the hot water heater. "I'm all right," she went on. "It's just hard to realize that Buck's sitting down there in the jailhouse now," she said. "He and I go back a long time."

Linda Sue was sitting at the kitchen table eating peanut butter and crackers. "Y'all grew up together, didn't you?" she asked.

"We went to school together until I quit in the eighth grade to go to work in the mill. Of course, he was a year younger than me, like Jonnie and Sonny are." Her eyes looked like they were seeing backward into those years.

"Your daddy's house was that little cracker box the Whitley's live in now, wasn't it?" I said.

"Yes, Buck and I lived eight houses apart just like you and Sonny."

"It's almost like reincarnation," I said but regretted it before the last word rolled off my bottom lip.

"Jonnie, you know I don't have much use for the discussions you girls have with your daddy about who some boy you see every day was in his other life back during the War Between the States." She frowned and reached past me to rub lard on the bottom of a biscuit pan.

"Sorry, I'll stick with the facts," I said. "Didn't Buck ride a bicycle up and down Gibson Street back then like Sonny does now?"

"Oh yes, and sometimes I was bouncing on his back fender too. When we were twelve or so, a boy his age wouldn't normally give a girl the time of day. I reckon I was such a skinny little tomboy, though, that he liked me or at least tolerated me."

Linda Sue came over, took the lid off the tomato noodles, and stirred them with a tablespoon. "But didn't he almost get you run over by a train one time?" She asked.

"Yes, he decided he'd outrace the 4:30 Southern one day after school. All I could do was hang on for dear life. We both heard its whistle before we reached the crossing in front of Harmony Mills Plant 6, but Buck didn't slow down in the least. When we hit the tracks, I flew two feet into the air, but I knew better than to turn loose of Buck's shirt tail. I bet the engineer cussed a blue streak when we went by."

"So Buck took risks, even back then?" I said.

"All young boys take risks, Jonnie. Some girls do too." She leveled a look at me, and I knew Daddy had told her about us almost shooting the man down across the railroad track yesterday.

I shaped my first biscuit and opened my hands for her to put her mark of approval on it.

She nodded and said, "That's a good one. I bet you'll make an *A* on this learning project. Could be you'll be making biscuits for Luke somewhere down the road."

Two weeks ago her words would've put a big smile on my face. The disagreements he and I'd had about Buck since the murder were still hanging in my mind though. And it didn't help any when the snow scared him and he brought me home early last Saturday night. Before I answered, I shaped another biscuit and placed it beside the first one in the greased pan. "I don't know," I said. "Sometimes we don't see eye to eye on things. This past week, it was lots of times."

"Don't forget that Mrs. Gilmore had been a leader in his church for years," she said.

Linda Sue had held her tongue as long as she could. "Don't forget that Buck has been our neighbor for years," she said. I cut my eyes over to her real quick. I thought she might have been too sassy for her own good that time.

Mama surprised me when she put her hand on my sister's shoulder for just a second and said, "Not just a neighbor, Honey, a friend. A mighty good friend."

Daddy came in with *The Telegram*. "What would Commodore Eudy say if he was alive today and knew his boy was accused of this awful crime?" he said.

"At least, Buck's got some help now," Mama answered. "If I was accused of murder or anything else, Clayton Wilkie's somebody I'd want on my side."

I saw my chance then. "Well, what y'all think about him asking me to help him out?" I asked. "I'll probably see some of the boys from the Tabernacle when I go out with Luke Saturday night."

"You won't be hearing anything important from that bunch," Linda Sue said, "because they don't know anything important. They got their two inches in *The Telegram* last week. That's it for them."

Daddy was going through the headlines in the paper, but he stopped and looked over toward Mama. I think he was trying to figure out how she felt about me helping the lawyer.

Mama inspected the ten biscuits I had put into the pan. "The middle one's too fat. Pinch some off it or it won't get done clear through," she said. "And as for helping Clayton Wilkie, you better let Sheriff Shepherd be the one that reports evidence in this case. You have your grades to keep up in school and your job at the dry cleaners to do on Saturdays. I don't see where you could find the time to be out doing detective work for the lawyer."

"Not unless you give up your one date a week with Luke." Linda Sue let loose one sharp laugh and put her hand over her mouth like a dozen more were trying to get out. Nobody even gave her a glance.

I remade my fat biscuit and moved to the preheated oven to do my baking. Daddy laid the paper down on the table and walked over to put his big hand on top of my hand that held the biscuit pan. "They look good, Jonnie. Ought to make for good eating at supper."

Then he grinned toward Mama and said, "Don't she remind you of my mama, Lois?"

"I reckon she does, John. But then, she's always been the spittin' image of you."

He kept his eyes on Mama and said, "I don't think it'll do no harm for her to snoop around a little for Lawyer Wilkie. I'm not saying there's any call for her to take time away from her studies or from her job at the dry cleaners. But when she meets up with these young people he's needing information from, she could surely ask them questions. I don't mind letting her use the Chevy to take anything she finds down to his office either. After all, it's for Buck's sake."

"Jonnie, put the biscuits in now. We're all getting hungry," Mama said. "Linda Sue, come turn off the noodles and watch these chicken legs so they won't burn." My sister had propped herself on the table and opened the last section of *The Telegram* to read the funnies.

"I know you're right, John," Mama finally answered. "We've backed him up more than one time when people on this side of town haven't. I remember when he finished high school and said he was going off to college. Many's the person up here on Mill Hill who gave him six weeks to get into enough trouble to be sent home. I think they looked forward to ribbing him when he had to come back and go to work in the mill for Mr. Davidson."

"Yeah, they didn't give him much of a chance," Daddy said.

Mama looked at me and smiled. "He fooled them though," she said. "He went way up into the mountains to Appalachian. That school was two hundred miles from this town and Gibson Street and Mr. Charlie Davidson's mill. And he stayed there the whole four years. He didn't even come home in the summer. Stayed up there working. But when he'd proved them all wrong and graduated, he came straight back home to Harmony to teach math and coach baseball at the same county high school he'd gone to himself."

She stopped and thought for a minute and then asked. "Are you timing your biscuits?"

"Yes. They've been in five minutes now," I answered.

She moved closer to me so that she could put her arm around my waist and give me a little hug. "I'll go along with your daddy this time," she said. "You go ahead and report anything you hear to Lawyer Wilkie. I 'spect you owe that much to Buck for all the times you've been over to his house when a math problem stumped you."

We both smiled.

Chapter 14

Demons in the Back Seat

Before church this morning, my daddy parked himself in the bathroom for an hour. He knows I have to comb my hair and put on my makeup in there every Sunday, but does he care? Oh no. First he steamed it up good shaving and taking a bath. Then to top it all off, he locked the door and stunk it up to high heaven before he said, "You're next, Jonnie."

Mama can hurry him without making him mad, but not me, so I went to her twice. She just looked at me like we had until noon to get ready and then said, "I don't know what's got you in such a state, Jonnie, but you've been ill as a hornet ever since you got out of bed.

If you can't wait your turn, use your own dresser mirror." The bathroom mirror is the only one in the house that has lights on each side. In the dresser mirror you can hardly see yourself, much less comb your hair and put on lipstick.

Truth be told, it was Luke Goodman I was mad at, not my daddy. We go out on a date every Saturday. He's been known to invite me to a cookout at his church on Friday night or to drop by my house to talk on Sunday afternoon, but usually Saturday night is it for us. On that one and only night, I always do what I can to make myself the prettiest girl he's seen all week. After I get home from my job at Purifoy's Cleaners, I pour Avon bubble bath into the tub and fill it with the hottest water I can stand. Then I soak for thirty minutes. I wear one of my sexiest outfits and brush my black hair till it shines. My complexion is the best thing I have going for me, but on Saturday night I use a little powder on my face, whether I need it or not. Just as I hear Luke's car come down the drive, I dab Tabu behind each ear.

Last night I checked myself in the mirror and smiled when I saw how well my efforts had paid off. My cream-colored skirt and vest and my new black jersey were just right for a downtown movie. Before Luke ever got close to my house, I'd made up my mind where we would go.

He was right on time. The two of us took a minute to walk back to the den where Mama and Daddy were watching *The Arthur Smith Show*. When I told them we were going downtown to see a movie, Luke looked like I'd just handed him a cow pie as a Christmas present.

"I was thinking we could go out to Baker's Lake to the Putt-Putt course," he said. "JB and the Peacock twins might be out there tonight."

As much as I despise the man's music, it still went through my mind that I'd rather watch Arthur Smith, the Charlotte hillbilly, with Mama and Daddy than go meet up with Luke's friends to play Putt-Putt. I bit my tongue, though, and said to Mama, "Well, we'll be at one of those places. Don't worry about us."

"You'll be back by eleven then?" she asked.

"Oh yes," Luke replied. "Probably before then."

I gritted my teeth but nobody noticed.

When we got into Luke's Ford, I said, "Don't crank it yet. Just sit here a minute."

He hadn't bothered to comment on how good I looked, but he looked at himself in the rearview mirror, used his right hand to smooth his blonde hair back behind his ear, and then let his eyes meet mine. "Okay," he said.

"I really want to go to that movie," I began. "Yesterday, at the end of my psychology class, Miss Stewart told us to try to get down to the Stanly Theater to see *I Want to Live* this weekend."

He frowned at me. "A theater that her daddy just happens to own," he said.

"What does that have to do with you and me going there tonight?" I asked.

"Nothing. Forget it."

"Then let's go see the movie." I crossed my arms and let my breath out hard. "She said it's based on a real case and comes off almost like a documentary about this doomed murderess' final days. It stars Susan Hayward. You know how much I like her."

"It's just not my idea of a good time. Why would you want to go watch a criminal sitting in a cell waiting for the gas chamber?" He looked at me like he thought I was the criminal.

"Hold it. I think I get it now," I said real low and slow. "It's going to bother you because you and your buddies put Buck Eudy in a jail. You know he might be headed for death row too."

His eyes told me I'd hit the nail on the head, but his mouth interrupted and disagreed. "It's not that at all."

"Well then, what is it?"

"I've told you before that I feel funny going to movies. Sister Gilmore used to tell us in youth meetings to steer clear of movies unless one came along that we wouldn't mind taking Jesus to see. Jesus is the last person I'd want to take to see Susan Hayward playing a woman who murdered her husband."

I kept my voice barely above a whisper. "Wonder if Mrs. Gilmore ever read about Jesus asking the Samaritan woman who'd had five husbands to give Him a drink of water? Then there was Mary Magdalene."

"Look, if you don't want to go play Putt-Putt, we'll go bowl a game. Did you cut out that coupon for free shoe rental that was in *The Telegram* last month?"

"No," I lied. I'd used it one Friday when Sonny, Linda Sue, and I had bowled together.

"Too bad, but at least I've got mine."

"I'll pay for my shoes." I gave him a hateful look.

"No, I didn't mean that. We'll go and I'll pay." He cranked the car. "It's probably too late to get to the movie before it starts anyway."

That's how we ended up at the bowling alley even though I was dressed for a movie date. I was so mad at him while we bowled that I pretended he was the head pin every time I threw the ball. I scored one hundred fifty-four and beat him by twenty-four pins.

Near the end of our game, Grady and Parks Peacock showed up. They'd been at the Putt-Putt, which is just a stone's throw away from the bowling alley, and had seen Luke's car in the parking lot. I welcomed them the same way I would welcome a swarm of blow flies to a Sunday picnic, but Luke invited them to join us. They sat down with us but claimed they didn't know the first thing about bowling. I breathed a sigh of relief and went right on throwing my ball down the alley toward the strike pocket but not caring when it veered too far to the left and whacked Head Pin Luke.

Each time Luke was up to bowl, I tried to pick the twins for information about Mrs. Gilmore's death. For some reason, Grady, Luke, and Billy Mack had hung around the church after the cookout that night long enough to see Buck throw down his broom and stomp out of the basement. I wondered if all three boys had told the same story about what they saw, and I thought Lawyer Wilkie might wonder too.

"I never heard why you were still at the church after most everybody else left the night Mrs. Gilmore was killed," I said to Grady.

"It didn't seem right to leave her to close up by herself," he answered and then nodded at his brother. "Parks took our car but I knew Luke would give me a ride. I just wish I'd stayed there until she got in her car and hit the road for home."

"What for?" Parks said. "Billy Mack walked to the parking lot with her. It didn't help."

"What happened between Mrs. Gilmore and Buck Eudy that night?" I asked Grady.

He sat there a minute and twisted the collar of his bright yellow shirt. Parks was about to answer for him when he said, "Well, she was a bossy person, and Buck was somebody you couldn't boss around. Maybe he got that way when he was a coach."

"I'm going to get me a Sundrop," Parks said. He left and I was glad of it. The twins can be a pill when they're together, but Grady, by himself, is easier to take. In fact, he's almost normal.

"Did both of them lose their tempers that night?" I asked.

"Yes, I guess that's the way you would put it. They lost their tempers. Buck had no business saying *hell* in the church, even if it was just the basement. I'll have to admit, though, she did come down hard on him." I could tell he was considering telling me more but wasn't sure he ought to. I just sat there giving him plenty of time.

"Sister Gilmore hadn't been herself the last month or so," he said. "It had come to the place that the least little thing got on her nerves. It didn't take nothing to make her fly off the handle. Something was bothering her, but I don't know what it was."

Luke finished his turn and sat down. He left the 7-10 split standing.

Without half aiming, I put my ball right in the pocket and got a strike. I was in a hurry to get back to Grady. I sat down real close to him so I wouldn't have to yell to be heard. "You're saying you think she was too quick to get mad at Buck about telling you boys to sweep up the basement?" I asked.

"Maybe. None of us woulda minded it at all. We like old Buck. Least we used to. He sure does know his baseball. Our softball team can use any help it can get, if you know what I mean. We ain't the Yankees."

"Did Buck look like he was going to hit her with the broom?"

"Oh no. He just lifted it into the air and then slammed it to the floor. Of course, then he spit tobacco juice right beside it. If I hadn't been so surprised, I mighta busted out laughing. It was kinda funny."

Luke finished his ninth frame. I had been too interested in what Grady was telling me to mark the score. He gave me a funny look and put a spare in the little box. I got up and rolled a spare myself.

We were coming up on the last frame. I had to talk fast. "Did Buck seem mad enough to kill Mrs. Gilmore?" I asked.

"Not at the time. I wouldn't ever have thought he'd come back and hurt her. I mean, I've seen my mama ten times madder at me and Parks than Buck was at her."

"So y'all left a few minutes after Buck stomped up the basement steps?"

"Me and Luke did, but Billy Mack stayed around. You know how he likes to play up to grownups. He told Sister Gilmore he'd help her carry her stuff to the car. We waited for them a few minutes at the top of the basement stairs, but then we went on to the parking lot. Billy Mack had his own car. He didn't need a ride."

"So Billy Mack just might have been the last one to see her before she was killed," I said.

"It seems that way."

"Was Buck's old truck in the parking lot?"

"No, but it mighta been in that little dirt lot behind the church. The sheriff asked us about that."

Luke sat down and started taking off his shoes. He'd left the five pin standing in the tenth frame and acted like he'd just as soon leave as watch me bowl my final frame. When I finished out my best game ever, I was disappointed to see Grady and Parks playing the pin ball machines near the snack bar. That ended my bloodhound work for the night. At least, I thought it did.

Luke didn't ask if I wanted to bowl another game, and I guess I know why. I sat eyeing the crowd while he went to turn in our bowling shoes. JB Blanton came out of the men's bathroom, saw me, and made for my seat. He didn't sit down in Luke's empty space, just stood looking down at me for a minute.

"Hey, JB," I said without smiling.

"Heard you think I got red paint on my hands," he said.

"What're you talking about?" I said. I looked for my boyfriend at the shoe counter. He was third in line.

"You know what I mean. Luke's been running his mouth about something that's none of his business."

I hate to be talked down to, so I stood up and frowned at him. "Did you or didn't you paint those nasty pictures of Mrs. Gilmore on the wall behind your church's choir loft?" My question surprised me but I kept frowning at him.

He grasped my upper arm and squeezed until I flinched. "You wouldn't believe me if I said I didn't. Right?" He squeezed again. I knew I'd have a bruise tomorrow.

I tried to twist out of his grip. "Turn me loose," I said and kicked his right ankle. He let go but made a fist and banged it on the table beside us. Somebody's Coke glass fell over and ice rolled out. "You want some of this?" he said, putting the fist under my nose.

I'll never know what my answer would've been. I looked toward the shoe counter again and saw Luke coming our way. JB's eyes followed mine. Then he took a couple steps backward. "You better lay off," he said. "You're just like Sister Gilmore. Always putting your nose where it doesn't belong." He took another step and backed into a table girl coming to wipe up his spill. He didn't bother

164

to apologize to her, just shot a warning at me before he made for the door. "And you know what happened to her."

Luke had seen me talking to his friend. "Where'd JB go?" he said. "Did you ask him to play a game of Putt-Putt with us?"

"Not on your life, I didn't. You couldn't pay me enough to play Putt-Putt with that hateful thing."

"Calm down, Jonnie. People are staring at you."

I lowered my voice a notch. "Like they were staring at your good buddy just now when he grabbed me by the arm and threatened me? He knew you'd told me about the nasty pictures and about him threatening you. How did that happen?"

He frowned. "If you want to know the truth," he said, "it's your fault."

I groaned and rolled my eyes. "How do you figure that?" I said.

"When I told you about it last Saturday night at the drive-in, it bothered you. You said he was threatening me that time I kidded him about not getting to date but once a week. You know—he told me to keep my mouth shut or I might find red paint on the back of my house too."

"Yes, but you had no right to mention my name to him."

"I'm getting to that. You asked me if I'd talked to JB about the pictures. I said I hadn't. The more I thought about what you'd said, the more my conscience bothered me. So next morning at church, I asked JB about the pictures."

"Okay, but I still don't see why you stuck me in the middle of it."

"To start with, I just talked about the murder. I asked him if he thought somebody other than Buck mighta killed Sister Gilmore. He wanted to know where I got that idea, and I told him from you."

"That's fine with me. I don't care how many people know that I believe Buck's innocent."

"One thing led to another, and he got madder and madder at me. I guess I wasn't thinking straight when I told him you knew about the drawings on the wall and about what you call his threat to paint stuff on my house. I said you thought the person who painted the pictures might be the same one who killed Sister Gilmore. He said tell you Buck Eudy could swing a paint brush just like he could swing a push broom."

"Sounds to me like you brought me into the argument so he'd have somebody besides you to be mad at. He let me know in no uncertain terms that he was mad at me." I lifted my arm and showed him the red marks JB's fingers had left. Here was Luke's chance to say *I'm sorry*.

"He does have a bad temper," he said.

"Yeah. People say the same thing about Buck Eudy," I answered and walked toward the bowling alley's glass doors.

It was a few minutes past nine o'clock. I thought Luke and I would go up to the Hum Dinger to get something to eat, but he didn't mention getting anything, not even so much as a drink. By half past

166

nine, we were back in my house. I sat him down on the living room couch. "I'm going to get us a drink," I said. "Be back in a minute."

Mama and Linda Sue were watching television in the den, and Daddy was asleep with the newspaper over his face. "Home early?" Mama said but didn't leave her program.

Linda Sue came across the den and stood in the kitchen door. She raised her eyebrows and said, "What happened to *I Want to Live?*"

"Don't ask," I said, trying to keep my voice level. "Later." She shrugged her shoulders as if she weren't interested, but I knew she was.

I poured Pepsi into two tea glasses and put some potato chips into a cereal bowl. Luke was leafing through my Grandma's Bible when I got back to the living room and set the tray of food and drinks on the coffee table.

"I like the way Jesus' words are printed in red letters in this Bible," he said.

"I love that Bible," I said, "because I know my grandma's hands touched its pages. But we need to put it back on the marble-top table where Mama keeps it. It belonged to her mama and she doesn't let us mess with it much."

I wanted my boyfriend to forget Grandma's Red Letter Edition for right now. I had decided to do something with what was left of this date. I closed both doors that connected the living room to the rest of the house and plopped myself on the sofa almost on top of him. I took his left hand in mine and put it on my right leg. The living room was chilly but I hoped my leg felt warm through my skirt.

"Well," he said. His face was surprised but he was smiling as he turned toward me on the stiff Duncan Phyfe sofa. He put his arm around my shoulders and kissed me on the mouth. His lips barely touched mine. It wasn't much better than kissing the 8X10 school picture he gave me last Christmas. He reached to get his drink off the coffee table, but I'd made up my mind that before the night was over, I would know what Luke Goodman had to offer. I put myself between him and his Pepsi and ended up lying on top of him, stomach to stomach, breast to chest.

"Now, you can really kiss me," I said, my mouth talking to his mouth, my eyes talking to his eyes. Our sexual parts were talking too, whether he wanted them to or not.

When he lifted his head to kiss me, I opened my mouth and dreamed of his tongue slipping between my lips like a velvet spoon. Nothing. So I moved my mouth to his ear and drew circles around its edge with my tongue. I used just the tip but made the circles smaller and smaller until I felt him tremble. He put both his arms around me and pulled me so close I could feel his warm hardness through his khakis. We kissed and rocked and moaned. My mind kept saying "Please don't stop. This is the way it should have been all along."

His hand untucked my black jersey and moved to cover my breast. I was so near the edge I thought I would scream and scream and scream. Daddy's mantle clock began to strike. Luke moved his right leg between my legs and rocked it in rhythm with the clock's striking. Oh God, could I wait for ten to sound?

I guess I'll never know the answer to that one. With the eighth strike, Luke pulled away from me, and by the tenth he was sitting bolt upright. "I've got to go home," he said as if he'd just seen a vision of his house exploding in the night.

"It's only ten. Why don't you stay till eleven?" I put my hand on his chin and played with his frown.

He stood up and took a comb out of his back pocket. He walked to the mirror over the mantle and moved his head back and forth as if he couldn't believe what he saw there. Finally, he combed every blond hair into place and then retucked his shirt into his pants. He turned and started for the front door but threw me a look as he opened it. "Be sure you straighten yourself up," he said. "Your hair's a mess."

"You coward," I said. But he was gone.

I walked to the bathroom and gave my hair a lick and a promise. Then I went back to the living room to put the sofa pillows in place and pick up the snacks we hadn't touched. Linda Sue was watching *Gunsmoke* in the den. I put fresh ice in the Pepsis, returned them to the tray, and joined my sister. "Party time," I said.

"Lukie Boy have an early curfew?" she asked.

"It's a long story," I said.

"I love a story." She got up from the floor and flicked off the TV.

"How many years you been watching *Gunsmoke*?" I asked.

169

"Oh, three. Maybe four."

"You ever seen the marshal kiss Miss Kitty?"

"Nope."

"Ever wonder why not? I mean he's a heck of a good looking guy, and she's got a figure that won't stop. There's something wrong there, Linda Sue. Something wrong, wrong, wrong."

Then I told her what had just happened between Luke and me, not every little detail but most of it. She interrupted a dozen times with questions and smart remarks, but when I finished, she said, "There's something wrong there, Jonnie. Something wrong, wrong, wrong."

The phone rang on her last *wrong*. I hurried to answer it before Mama could wake up and stumble out of the back bedroom.

"Hello." *An apology*, I thought.

Linda Sue had followed me to the kitchen. "Luke?" she whispered. When I nodded my head yes, she sat down at the kitchen table to listen.

"Jonnie, I need to tell you what happened to me on the way home," he said in a nervous voice.

An accident was the first thing that popped into my mind. I could see cuts and blood on his handsome face. "Are you all right, Luke?"

"I am now, but let me tell you all of it."

"Okay. Go ahead." It didn't look like this was going to turn out to be an apology after all.

"Did you hear it thundering in the distance before I left your house?"

"No, and I didn't feel the earth move either." My sarcastic remark was wasted on him. He's never read a Hemingway novel in his life.

"I'm not joking." He was almost hateful. "I heard it thundering around ten o'clock."

"I remember hearing the clock strike ten." I waited for him to take the bait. When he didn't, I decided to let him tell whatever he had to tell. "I know it's raining now. Did your tires skid on the road?"

"No, I wasn't in an accident. Now listen. When I got in my car beside your house, I didn't feel right. The air inside was warm, almost hot. It was heavy too. It felt like it was weighing down my shoulders."

"Why didn't you just roll down the windows?"

"I wanted to but it started to rain so I couldn't."

Snow spooked him last weekend. This weekend, it's rain. "Maybe you're getting the flu or something," I said.

"No, it's not the flu. Listen. I cranked the car and began to back up your driveway, but I had to slam on my brakes before I got to the top. Something was up there beside the road at your mailbox."

"What do you mean *something*?" I broke in. "Was it Buck's big dog Willie? Since we've been feeding him, he wanders over to our house right often."

"No, it wasn't a dog. It wasn't even on the ground. You're not going to believe this, but a bunch of faces were hanging over the top of your mailbox."

"Faces?" He was right. I didn't believe his tale.

"Yeah, but it was just for a minute. When I hit my brakes, a big flash of lightning lit up the sky and made me shut my eyes tight. When I opened them, the faces were gone. I'm not even sure I really saw them hanging there in the first place."

"It might've been Buck's ball players," I said into the receiver. "Remember, they were on his front porch last Saturday night when we came home early in the snow."

"They didn't look like any ball players I ever seen," he said. "But there's more."

I have to admit he had my attention.

"I got the car out of your driveway as fast as I could and started down the street. The longer I drove, the hotter it got. It was hard to breathe too. I felt like the Ford was full of demons and they were breathing up all the air. I didn't see anything but I could tell they were there."

This was the same boy who couldn't understand what I was talking about when I explained that my English teacher told us some of the things we can't see are just as important as those we can see. I wonder if he'd understand now.

"What did you do, Luke?"

"When I got to the bottom of the hill on Gibson Street, I pulled over to the curb and cut off the motor. I rolled down both windows and said as loud as I could, 'In the name of the Lord Jesus Christ, demons leave this car.' They left. I felt them leave."

I breathed in a long breath and then let it out again. If Luke had sat beside me these last eight months in Miss Belle Stewart's psychology class, I might have tried to talk to him about guilt complexes, schizophrenic tendencies, and fear of intimacy. If he didn't think the sun rose and set on the Deliverance Tabernacle of Faith, I might have reminded him how wrong a bunch of folks from his church were one night at a brush arbor meeting years ago when they thought they saw Jesus coming back to Earth in a big ball of fire. If he hadn't been so tangled up in the kind of religion the Gilmores had dished out for the past eight years, I might have explained to him how normal it was to swap hot kisses on a living room couch.

As it was, I just said, "I'm glad you got rid of those demons, Luke. Me, I've never seen any such things. I tell you one thing though. You just might be as crazy as Buck Eudy, who sees FBI agents coming up the railroad tracks." I said it in a voice so calm it sounded like I was telling him the time of day, and then I hung up.

Chapter 15

The Sugar Daddy

Tonight after young people's meeting at our church, I asked Sonny if he wanted to ride up to the Hum Dinger to get a drink. I didn't have to ask twice. As we crossed the parking lot to the Chevy, Linda Sue trailed behind. Sonny surprised me when he opened my door and held it while I got in.

"Are you buttering me up or something?" I asked.

"Don't tell me that boyfriend of yours don't open doors for you?" He cocked his head to one side and almost closed one of his brown eyes.

"That's different," I answered.

"You think so?" He shut my door and walked around the car. He met Linda Sue about to get in the front seat. "Mind if I sit up front?" he asked her. It was almost dark so Sonny didn't see me raise my eyebrows.

"You know as well as I do there's not room for three people up front," my sister said. "But you'll have plenty of room back there." She stabbed her finger toward the back seat and he crawled in.

Linda Sue started jabbering about how the Presbyterian Church across the street from ours serves refreshments after young people's meetings. She wondered why the mothers in our church didn't take turns making hot dogs or spaghetti for Trinity's young people. I ignored her complaints. Sonny sat in the back seat and didn't open his mouth during the ten-minute drive.

Clem Ketner never carhops at the Hum Dinger on Sunday nights. When we pulled up to the curb and I tooted the horn for service, Sonny said something about it being against Clem's religion to do stand-up work on Sunday nights. I'd heard the same joke from too many boys to laugh at it this time. His words just hung in the air like they wanted out but couldn't find an open window.

Selma Clinkscale takes Clem's place on his night off. Since she also works in the mill and sings in the choir at the Tabernacle, I don't know why she wants this job too. I'm always a little surprised to see her dressed in her black and maroon carhop outfit on Sunday nights. If the Gilmores had ever dropped by the Hum Dinger for a cheeseburger after a Sunday night preaching service, Selma would probably have ended up being the subject of a sermon.

She came sashaying down the sidewalk to take our order. I swear, she and Clem must have gone to the same hip-swinging classes. He has twice as much meat on his bones, but that's about the only difference in their walks.

"What you sweethearts want tonight?" Her red lips glowed in the neon lights.

"We'll take three Pepsis, Mrs. Clinkscale." It always seems funny to call her that when she comes up to the car, but Mama taught Linda Sue and me to use respect when we speak to adults.

"Coming up, Miss Sparks." She winked at me and left.

Most times Sonny would've wisecracked about her after she walked off, but he didn't say a word as she left tonight. Maybe because we'd ignored his joke about Clem's stand-up job.

After a minute or so he said, "So what you heard about the murder this week?"

Linda Sue turned half way around in the seat and announced, "Jonnie's snooping for Lawyer Wilkie now. Gonna see what she can find out from Luke Good Man and his buddies."

I glared at her for a minute and then looked over my shoulder at Sonny and said, "Come on up here with us. I don't like having to crane my neck around to talk to you." Linda Sue opened her mouth, ready to spit out a sarcastic remark, but I rattled the car keys and she thought better of it.

"Open the door and let Sonny out of the back seat before Selma gets back with our drinks," I told her. "If you don't want to ride the hump, he can sit in the middle." She got out of the car but

176

took her own good time doing it. She tilted the seat forward and stood beside the door while Sonny got out. Then she bowed like a chauffeur and watched him crawl into the front and slide across the seat. It was a tight fit. Our legs touched.

"You found out anything worth telling him yet?" His voice cracked. I could tell he was nervous.

"Luke is so close-lipped that I'll never learn anything from him," I said, "but I plan to pass on something Grady Peacock mentioned at the bowling alley last night."

Selma arrived with our order and hooked the tray over my open window. "Thirty cents, Miss Sparks." While the three of us fished dimes out of our pockets, she waited with one hand on her hip and one on the tray. I found an extra nickel for a tip, put the coins on her tray, and passed drinks to Sonny and Linda Sue.

Selma raked the money into her palm. "Thanks, kids," she said and then bent down so she could see all of us through the window. "I'm saving all my tips for a train ticket to the Big Apple. I'll send you a postcard when I go for my audition in a hundred years or so." She unhooked the tray and moved off toward a bright yellow Edsel that was blaring its horn about six spaces past us.

"She does have a good singing voice," I said. "She sang at Mrs. Gilmore's funeral."

"You were about to tell me what you found out from Tweedle-De-Dum's brother at the bowling alley," Sonny said.

"According to Grady, Mrs. Gilmore hadn't been herself these past few months. He thinks something was bothering her." I had more to say but Linda Sue butted in.

"From what I hear, that woman was a grouch half the time anyway. Why tell Lawyer Wilkie something that's common knowledge to every member of the Deliverance Tabernacle of Faith?"

"Because you never know when a little piece of information might lead to something important," I said. I had no more than gotten the words out of my mouth when they caused a nasty red picture of Mrs. Gilmore to float up in my mind. A person wearing a stocking over his face stood beside the drawing. In one hand he held a brush with red paint dripping from its bristles. *Uh oh*, I thought. *Luke Goodman and I are pretty sure JB Blanton was mad enough at Mrs. Gilmore to paint those pictures on the back wall of the church. A little piece of evidence.*

My sister cleared her throat. The noise caused my picture to disappear. "You're going to blow up at me for saying this, Jonnie, but you know that there's one more story that hasn't been told yet."

Two more stories, I thought.

"What you saw at the day camp might not have a thing to do with the murder." she went on, "but you can't tell me there wasn't something wrong out there. Bad wrong. Anyway, it's the nuttiest thing I've ever heard come out of Luke's church."

"Is this the story I'm never supposed to mention again?" Sonny asked.

I put my fingertips up to my temples and bit on my bottom lip. Luke had been so sure there was nothing wrong going on that afternoon, but I decided I'd kept quiet long enough.

I nodded at Sonny. "Yup," I said, "and Linda Sue's right. If I'm going to snoop around looking for things that might help Lawyer Wilkie, I guess it's time I put my own story in his hands too."

"Wanna try it out on me first?" He knew the answer before he asked the question.

"I'm the only one she's told so far," Linda Sue blurted out.

"Okay, I'm going to tell you now, Sonny, and then I'm going home to tell Mama and Daddy. Clayton Wilkie will get it tomorrow, but I'm still not sure how it could connect to the murder." I knew I had two stories to give the lawyer, but one was all I was ready to tell Sonny tonight..

"Now you're talking." I don't think Sonny would've been happier if I'd handed him the key to my five-year diary.

"You know Luke worked in that day camp his church ran last summer," I began.

"Yeah."

"Well, one day about five o'clock, his mama called me and explained in that sweet little voice of hers that she couldn't go pick up Luke after work because they'd had trouble with their Ford."

A car full of girls pulled in beside us and honked for Selma. Sonny's eyes didn't leave my face.

"Daddy let me take our car way out in the country five miles past their church to pick up Luke at the camp. I got there thirty minutes early and had no more idea where Luke might be than the man in the moon. The road dead ended into a clearing in the woods. To the right I saw two shelters with no walls. Behind them was a ball field of sorts where a bunch of little boys were throwing a softball around. I didn't see a counselor or anything. To the left stood three log buildings, none of them of much size. Behind them was a muddy lake. I wondered what kinds of snakes swam with the campers. A lot of racket was coming from one of the log buildings so I decided to try my luck there.

"I knocked on the door, but the giggling and shrieking inside drowned it out. I pushed it open a little bit. The room must have been Rev. Gilmore's office. He was sitting on one of those swivel chairs close to a desk and wearing a dripping-wet green bathing suit. Four little boys—naked as the day they were born—sat on wet towels on the floor. All of them were licking Sugar Daddies. Rev. Gilmore turned round and round in his chair, holding Sugar Daddies up above his head while three more naked boys chased after them screaming, 'Mine, mine, mine.'"

We heard a knock on the Chevy's metal top and all of us jumped. Selma stood beside my window. "You sweethearts want anything else?" she asked.

"No, we're just sitting here talking," I answered.

"You oughta come to church with Luke next Sunday, Jonnie. Brother Gilmore's promised to be back in the pulpit that morning. First time since Sister Gilmore passed away. I know he'll give us something to think about."

I swallowed hard. "Thank you for inviting me, Mrs. Clinkscale. I might take you up on it," I mumbled.

"Fine. See you then, Shug." She turned and left.

"Get back to Rev. Gilmore and the day camp boys," Sonny said. "This story's sure as hell giving *me* something to think about."

"How do you think *I* felt as I stood there froze in my tracks watching him and the little boys? I never saw anything like it before or since. While I watched, Rev. Gilmore slowed his turning enough that two of the screaming boys were able to scramble onto his lap. They tried to climb up his chest, but they were wet and kept slipping. He laughed at them and called them slippery eels. Finally, he let them have their Sugar Daddies, and they joined the boys on the floor.

"Then he turned his attention to a little boy who was sitting in the corner looking like he was about to cry. 'Don't worry, Jimbo,' he said. 'There's one left for you. I'll even unwrap it. All you have to do is climb up Sugar Mountain to get it.'"

"Holy hell!" Sonny exploded. "How long have you known this?"

"Just wait. She's not finished," Linda Sue said.

"That littlest one—it was Jimbo Folks, Carl and Linda's baby—he scrambled up and grabbed the Sugar Daddy and sat smack dab in the middle of Rev. Gilmore's chest licking it. The preacher has a big sunken hole there. That's where Jimbo plopped his bottom."

Sonny's mouth dropped open. For a couple seconds he just sat shaking his head. Then he said, "I ain't believing this."

"You can believe it," Linda Sue said. "Go on, Jonnie."

181

"Next, Rev. Gilmore smiled down at Jimbo sitting like a baby bird in a bird nest and said, 'Here, it's too big for you to handle all by yourself. Let me help you lick it.'"

"Shit. And him a preacher."

"Yes, and him a preacher. And that's what he was doing when I felt a hand grab my waist and shove me so hard I lost my balance and fell off the porch. It was Mrs. Gilmore and she was fit to be tied. While I was on the ground, she flung the door wide open and stomped in. I can't tell you what happened next in that office because I wasted no time getting over to the other building, collecting Luke, and getting out of there."

"And you haven't told anybody?"

"Except me." Linda Sue pointed at her chest with both index fingers.

"Yes, I told Linda Sue, of course, and I told Luke on the way over to the service station where we had to pick up his daddy and their car."

"What did he say?"

I screwed my mouth into a frown. "He told me I was making a mountain out of a molehill. He said Brother Gilmore has a way with boys, that he charms little boys just like some people charm snakes."

"You're kidding."

"Nope."

"What did his daddy say?"

"Oh, Luke told me not to mention it to his daddy because he didn't want him to think I was silly. So that was that."

"Well, if that don't beat all."

"Now, I don't want you to breathe a word of this to anybody until Lawyer Wilkie has had a chance to pass judgment on it. Okay?"

"If you say so, but I don't see why you've kept that story under a lid."

"It's 'cause Luke Goodman told her to. Whatever he tells her, she does," Linda Sue said. "She thinks he's so great, but all he is is good looking."

"That smart remark means you get to be let out first, Miss Priss." I started the car before she could complain.

When I stopped in front of our house, I said, "You're sitting on the door side. Get on out and then I'll take Sonny home. Tell Mama I'll be back in ten minutes, and don't tell her anything else. Understand?"

"Okay, but I still say Luke Goodman's not so great." She flipped her pony tail and opened the door.

"You just might be right about that, Little Sister. Now get out."

Sonny slid over and we drove to his house. He could have walked, of course. He did it all the time. But I had my own reasons for driving him. After all, he had held the car door for me in the church parking lot before we went up to the Hum Dinger. I stopped by the curb in front of his house but he wasn't ready to get out. "I've heard stories from out at the Tabernacle myself," he said, "but none of them hold a candle to that one."

We were quiet for a minute.

"I 'preciate you telling me about the boys at the day camp," he said at last. "And boyfriend or no boyfriend, you need to tell some grownups."

"Yeah, I know it."

"Your boyfriend was a counselor out there all summer. Wonder what all he saw."

"No telling," I answered.

"I'll tell you this," he said. "If I was a counselor and one day I saw the preacher playing the Sugar Daddy game with a lap full of naked boys, the next day I wouldn't be no counselor."

"Me neither. I'm going home to tell Mama and Daddy right now."

Sonny opened the door and got out. He leaned over so he could see me through his open door. "See you tomorrow after school," he said.

"Sure," I answered. We've never made a habit of seeing each other on weekdays. I thought about that all the way home.

Mama and Daddy were sitting in the den, but Linda Sue had gone on into our bedroom, probably peeved because I'd dropped her off early. Daddy was flipping through the March *Readers Digest,* and Mama was pasting S&H Green Stamps into her little book. She's saving to get a toaster, even though the rest of us like the way she makes toast in the oven now. If you ask me, Mama just wants a toaster because Pearl Calloway got her one with Green Stamps and can't stop talking about how easy it is to use it. I need to ask Sonny just how much he likes the toast that comes out of his mama's new toaster.

Linda Sue must have heard the door shut when I came in because she was in the den in less time than it takes Elvis to say *hound dog.*

I hated having to tell Mama and Daddy the day camp story, but I knew there was no getting around it. Sex is something you have a hard time bringing up to your parents. Years ago Linda Sue talked me into asking Mama how babies get made, and we've come up with maybe half a dozen other questions since then. But I would no more talk to Daddy about sex than I'd ask Luke to stop at a drug store on Friday night so I could buy me a box of Kotex.

Finally, I sat down and told them everything I could remember about what had happened that afternoon, but I didn't mention sex. Better to let them come to their own conclusions. Of course, Linda Sue was quick to put in anything I left out, but she was like me, smart enough to steer clear of sex. They asked all the questions I'd thought they would. Why didn't you say anything to us when it happened? Who have you told? What did Luke say?

Neither one of them said anything about what they thought the whole thing meant. Maybe they weren't sure. I know I wasn't. I'm still not.

"Well, it won't do to keep this story to ourselves any longer," Mama said.

"You've got to go to the sheriff," Daddy said.

Mama put her hand up and rested her chin in it like what she had on her mind was almost too heavy to carry. "But we don't want to stir up a hornets' nest unless we're pretty sure the preacher's guilty of doing something he's got no business doing," she said. She always gives a person the benefit of a doubt. "That man and that church have a heap of trouble already. Before we open our mouths to Tubby Shepherd, we need to know we're doing the right thing."

All four of us sat there for a minute letting her words sink in. Linda Sue looked like she wanted to say something, but for once, she held her tongue. "I need to send Lawyer Wilkie a note about what I found out at the bowling alley Friday night," I said. "I was thinking I could pass this story by him at the same time."

The worry wrinkles between Mama's eyes relaxed. "That's just the thing, Jonnie," she said. "He'll know what you ought to do about it."

"One more day can't make a big difference," Daddy agreed. "We can drop your note at his office on our way to the mill tomorrow morning."

So that's exactly what I did. Except for one thing.

I called Luke Goodman too. Last summer when it happened, he had one chance to shed some light on what I'd witnessed. I wanted to give him another one now. I didn't want to take care of this business on the telephone, so I told him I needed to talk about a decision my family had just made that might mean the sheriff would want to question him again. Then I dropped the receiver on the floor, pushed down the button to break the connection, and stood there listening to the beep signaling that the receiver had been left off the hook.

In less than twenty minutes, he and I were sitting on the living room sofa. Just two nights ago, we'd made out hot and heavy on that same sofa. Of course, that was before he saw his vision at the end of our driveway. No telling what he'd see tonight after I hit him with the day camp story.

I figured I needed to look him straight in the eye, so I stood and paced up and down Mama's maroon rug a couple times. Then I pulled the rose velvet chair up close to the sofa, sat down, and got right to the point. "When you were a little boy, did you ever run around naked playing games with Rev. Gilmore?"

I'd caught him off guard. He opened his mouth several times but nothing came out. I just stood there staring into his blue eyes.

"Where in the world—" he said. "What makes you think—" The last word came out a croak like he was fourteen years old and his voice was beginning to change. Finally, he was able to say, "I can't believe you'd ask me such a thing."

"Well, did you?"

"No, I didn't," he said, "but what if I had?" His mouth turned down in a frown. I wondered if he meant it as a warning.

I curled and uncurled my fingers, not knowing how much I should say. "In all my years going to my church camp up in the mountains, we never ran around naked chasing lollipops. Of course, I was a Methodist and my counselors were college students from Catawba, but I think church camps ought to be about the same, no

matter what denomination runs them." I swallowed and scrunched my
eyes shut for a few seconds before I went on. "The picture of Jimbo
Folks crawling naked up Rev. Gilmore's belly after a Sugar Daddy
will never leave my mind." There, I'd got it out.

A blush started somewhere below the collar of Luke's blue
shirt and worked its way up his neck. In less than ten seconds, his face
looked like he'd been at Baker's Lake all day without using a drop of
Coppertone.

"I tell you one thing," he said, "you better not go out in
Harmony spreading a tale to make Brother Gilmore look like
something's wrong with him." He was breathing heavy. "Because it's
not so."

"Are you sure it's not?" I didn't give him a chance to answer.
"Suppose you come up on your own daddy some evening after he gets
home from work and changes into Bermuda shorts to mow the grass.
Let's say it's hot as blue blazes, so he strips off his shirt and
undershirt to finish up the yard. Then he returns the lawnmower to the
storage shed in your backyard, and that's where you surprise him
sitting in an old chair waving Sugar Daddies in the air and begging
your brother Sammy and his buddy J. Paul to climb up his sweaty
chest."

I quit then and waited.

He looked like he could've jumped right through me. "My
daddy's not the kind of man to do something like that," he said.

"So when did Rev. Gilmore get to be that kind?" I snapped. "You said it never happened when you were a camper. When did it start?"

He lowered his head and sat there quiet for a minute. Then he looked up and leaned forward on the sofa. Some other time, I might've thought he was fixing to kiss me, but this time I was sure he had no such idea in his head.

"There's no reason in the world for me to answer that question," he said.

"Why not, Luke?"

"Just like there's no reason for me to sit on this couch another minute."

"But Luke, you need to think about—"

"And for that matter, there's no reason for me ever to sit here again." He got up and started for the front door.

I held my breath. My heart was beating way too hard. Halfway across the room, he stopped, and I thought he was about to say something else. All he did, though, was glance at himself in the mirror hanging over the mantel and then leave without looking around.

Chapter 16

Piece by Piece

I lay awake for an hour this morning before time to get up for breakfast. Linda Sue was taking more than her half of the bed and snoring, but not loud. I tried counting sheep but my mind kept drifting off to special dates I'd had with Luke Goodman. Every one of them had a stinger hooked onto the end of it.

Take the Sweetheart Banquet in February, for instance. Only juniors and seniors from Harmony High are allowed to go, but they can invite a date from another school. I was really looking forward to going to my first banquet with my first steady boyfriend. My cousin Kay let me borrow the white chiffon semi-formal dress she wore to her senior prom last year. I washed all the starch out of two of my old crinoline petticoats and wore them under it so the skirt stood out just right. I felt like a princess.

First, we ate chicken breasts and mashed potatoes in the cafeteria while we listened to the glee club sing songs like "Let Me Call You Sweetheart" from my mama's day. Next, Mr. White got up and invited us all to dance. The loud speaker made a noise that sounded like somebody trying to start a motorcycle, but finally "Blue Suede Shoes" came out loud and clear. I put my hand on Luke's and smiled a big one at him. Nothing. He got up and went to the bathroom.

The people at the Tabernacle don't shag. Neither do they slow dance. It wouldn't surprise me if they decided moving your hips to keep a hula hoop turning would send you straight to Hell.

I let my mind move on to last summer at the lake. Luke's day camp job had ended because school was about to start. He asked me to help him baby-sit his little brother Sammy one day while his mama drove over to Salisbury to visit her uncle in the Veteran's hospital. I remember it was so hot your clothes stuck to you when you went outside. I had a brainstorm and suggested we pack a picnic lunch and go out to Baker's Lake. Luke liked the idea and Sammy nearly flipped when he found out we were taking him swimming.

Just after noon I unwrapped our baloney sandwiches and carrot sticks and put them on a cement table near the lake. We couldn't find any chairs but nobody minded standing. Luke fed three dimes into the drink box and pulled out Cokes for the two of us and a

Brownie Chocolate for Sammy. The sandwiches went fast. I'd made us a bunch of peanut butter crackers to eat after we had some time to swim, but I knew it wouldn't do to mention them until later. Sammy's like every ten year old on this Earth. *Wait* is the one four-letter word they don't understand.

We cleared our table and returned our bottles to the wire rack beside the drink box. Then we spread the Harmony Mills towels we'd brought from home on the sand near the lake. Sammy wanted to go on in. He'd been in such a hurry to swim that he'd left all the carrots for Luke and me and run over to stick his big toe in to test the water temperature. I made him hold still long enough for me to rub some baby oil mixed with iodine into his shoulders. It beats Coppertone if you want to get a dark suntan.

He dashed toward the wooden pier, held his nose, and jumped in feet first. Luke and I looked at each other and laughed. The sparkle in his blue eyes caused my heart to speed up. We watched Sammy and a gang of little boys fight over three black inner tubes Mr. Baker had put out for kids to use. It felt good to be sitting in the sun with the best looking boy at the lake, maybe the best looking boy in Harmony. The warm sun on my back made me want to touch Luke.

Getting up on my knees, I said, "Here, let me put some of this on your back." I uncapped the baby oil again. "Lie down on your towel so I can reach you."

He looked at me for a second, then frowned and said, "I don't use that stuff."

"Okay then, I'll lie down and you rub some on me." I looked into eyes that had lost their sparkle and tried to make him feel what I felt. "To tell the truth, I'd rather have your hands on me than mine on you." I handed him the oil and gave him a smile that would've moved many a boy I know.

It moved Luke Goodman all right. His face turned red under his suntan. He jumped up and threw the oil back to my towel. "I'm burning up," he said. "Didn't we come out here to swim?" He hit the water before I had time to answer. One more sting. Luke can be more dangerous than my daddy's honeybees.

Linda Sue broke into my bad memories with a loud snore. I gave her a little jab in the ribs so that she'd roll over on her side. I knew I'd seen my last wink of shut-eye for the night and thought about getting up. I felt like a big jigsaw puzzle hung from the ceiling above my head. Piece by piece, I was taking it apart. And I wasn't even trying to put it back together again.

I remembered how Luke ruined that March night before Easter when it snowed at the drive-in. All he thought about was how quick he could get me home. If having a snowball fight at the Starlite Drive-in is the biggest trouble he's ever got to face, I don't think he's got a whole lot to worry about.

My mind moved on to the demons he'd had to chase out of his car after we made out on the sofa last Saturday night. I couldn't think about that one without gritting my teeth.

I was glad when Mama stuck her head through the bedroom door at 6 AM and said, "It's Monday morning, girls. Come on now. Get up."

Linda Sue let out one more snore as my feet hit the floor. I walked across to the dresser and smiled at myself in the mirror. "You're never going to end up Mrs. Luke Goodman," I told my reflection. Then I wiped the sleep out of my eyes and said, "And that's okay, Jonnie Sparks."

At the breakfast table, Linda Sue wanted to talk about the fuss I had with Luke last night, but I got her quiet before Mama or Daddy overheard. It wasn't that I minded them knowing Luke was gone, maybe gone for good. It was just that I didn't have time to talk right then. I had more important things to do.

While I gobbled my eggs, I thought about the important note I needed to write. Mama didn't say a word when I left the table without finishing my toast or milk. I printed half a page, signed my name, and added a PS telling Lawyer Wilkie to call me for details after school today. At 11 AM, he was standing outside my English classroom door.

Mr. White said the principal had notified him in advance and that it was perfectly all right for me to miss his class. He handed me a piece of paper with notes about today's class work written on it. The lawyer and I went downstairs and sat at a table in the empty cafeteria. I spilled almost everything I knew, and you better believe Lawyer Wilkie took it serious. He filled a whole bunch of pages in his yellow legal pad.

After we finished, I asked him if I'd helped Buck's case. He scratched his nearly-bald head before he answered. "Jonnie," he said, "your story about the preacher and the little boys has made me add one more name to my list of people who might have killed Eunice Gilmore." He leaned his head to one side and thought for a minute. "You weren't the only one to witness the preacher taunting the naked boys with Sugar Daddies," he said. "I wonder what went on between him and his wife after she shoved you off the porch."

"As mad as she was that day, you can bet she didn't take him under her wing and protect him like she did Red," I answered.

"Your friend Luke ought to have information to add to the day camp story. He worked with those same boys that Rev. Gilmore did. We'll need to question him about the preacher's behavior. He might be willing to tell an old sheriff or an old lawyer a few things he was too embarrassed to tell his girlfriend. I'll get with Sheriff Shepherd. Whether it helps free Buck or not, the information belongs in the sheriff's hands."

I nodded my head slowly. Even though the story had never set easy in my mind, I knew Luke would be mad as all git-out when he found out I'd told it.

"The sheriff already knows about the vandalism done to the Tabernacle wall," the lawyer said. "He learned about it when he questioned Elder Humpy Barrier after the murder. There's nothing new in your account, but that incident should have been reported back in the winter when it happened."

His words bothered me. I was still holding onto details. I'd mentioned the pictures, but I hadn't told him that JB threatened Luke and me about them. My promise to Luke whispered in my memory. *"Jonnie, you can't say a word about this to anybody. Okay?"*

I'd answered, *"Okay."*

The lawyer went on listing his suspects. "Early on, I thought Red Byerly behaved very suspiciously when he disappeared for three days after Mrs. Gilmore's body was discovered. He said he didn't return to the church building to go to bed until 11 PM on the night of the murder and that the sheriff's car scared him off. But who's to say he wasn't there earlier, early enough to kill her?"

"I can't think of any reason Red would kill the very woman who'd taken pity on him and given him a place to sleep."

"Yes, motive, or the lack of it, is the reason Buck is sitting in the jail and Red is walking around on the outside and working at Buck's old job."

"What about his daddy?" I asked. "He admits he was at the Tabernacle close to the time Mrs. Gilmore was killed. If you ask me, he picked a mighty late hour to go collect room and board from Red."

"Right," he agreed, "and I understand he held a grudge against the preacher's wife because she did him out of the money he expected Red to turn over to him every time he did an odd job at the Tabernacle. Yes, the old man deserves another look."

"Don't forget the bucket of red paint I saw spilled in Archie's barn that Sunday," I said. "Archie Byerly could've put those pictures on the church wall."

196

"Yes, but you know both the Byerlys paint." He frowned and pulled on his floppy left jowl. "A young person is more likely to have painted those vulgar pictures. A grown man, especially a drunk like Archie, would have been more destructive."

I knew what I had to do then and I did it. "Red Byerly had nothing to do with those pictures," I heard myself say. "It was a young person who drew them all right, but not him."

How does it feel to fall out of love with someone? Does it happen all at once like love at first sight does? Or does it happen piece by piece until you finally realize it's all gone? I gave Lawyer Wilkie the whole story Luke had made me promise not to tell. How JB told Luke he'd better keep his mouth shut about his daddy cutting his dates down to one a week or he might find red paint on the back of his house. How JB threatened me at the bowling alley Saturday night. The lawyer said JB might be guilty of much more than a half dozen dirty pictures painted on a church wall. He will see that the sheriff questions JB.

Jonnie, you can't say a word about this to anybody. Okay?

I'd broken my promise, but I felt relieved, not guilty. That's when I knew for sure it was over for Luke and me.

Chapter 17

The Sherlock Streak

As I entered my office this morning, I stepped on a folded sheet of notebook paper. My clients don't write me notes over the weekend. *Jonnie Sparks,* I thought and smiled. First, she reported that a youngster from the Tabernacle told her the Gilmore woman had gotten real grumpy in recent months. That agrees with what Jaybird Blanton said at the Pig last Tuesday. Next, she said her boyfriend, a member at the Tabernacle, told her someone had drawn caricatures of Mrs. Gilmore on a church wall recently. Most important, she claimed to have witnessed Reverend Gilmore doing things at the Deliverance Tabernacle's day camp that no preacher has any business doing. *No preacher has any business doing.* Those were the words she had penned so neatly on her note.

I'd intended to get out to the Tabernacle this morning with some questions for the Reverend, but something about that note made me decide to go to Harmony High School and talk to Jonnie first. Maizie would call that my Sherlock streak. My Sherlock streak paid off. Jonnie had plenty to tell.

After I left the high school at noon, I returned to my office and dialed Tubby Shepherd. Irene Reid, who could take over the sheriff's job tomorrow if he dropped dead today, answered. Checking her boss' calendar, she informed me he was out until late afternoon and wouldn't reveal his whereabouts. "Tell me what you got, Lawyer," she said. "I'll get it to him the minute he comes through the door."

"No, you just put my name in the 4 PM slot, and let him know I have important news," I replied. The sheriff ought to deputize the woman.

Although Maizie packed my lunch this morning, I had a legitimate reason to eat elsewhere. Like me, Tubby loves Mabel's barbecue. I hoped I'd find him at the Pig. Maizie's brown bag contained an egg salad sandwich and two oatmeal cookies. The cookies would save, so I put them in a desk drawer. The sandwich, I tossed into a large trashcan in Mabel's parking lot.

A quick look through the plate-glass window told me the sheriff wasn't there. I went in anyway and parked myself beside Emerson Perkins. "You having any luck piecing together a defense for Buck Eudy?" he asked.

"Yes," I said. There's not enough concrete evidence to convict him. I think the worst he's guilty of is a bad temper."

I was relieved when Mabel came over with her little pad and pencil to take my order. What I'd learned from Jonnie this morning would have interested Emerson, but I didn't want to divulge a word of it yet. I ordered a barbecue sandwich with fries on the side and asked Emerson about the big after-Easter sale going on at Belk's. He bit my hook and described the buys in the men's department until my food arrived. I ate it but didn't linger long enough for Emerson to persuade me to visit Belk's and make a purchase from him.

The information I had wouldn't let me sit still waiting for my appointment with Tubby. After lunch I returned to my office and called Rev. Earl Gilmore. He agreed to see me and by half past one I was traveling Highway 42-A on my way to the Deliverance Tabernacle of Faith. Out of curiosity, I drove on past the church to take a look at the Gilmore residence, which is in walking distance of the church. The house appears to have five rooms. A garage with no door stands ten or fifteen feet away from it. Neither house nor garage is noteworthy, except for one thing. Both are painted a sick green that appeals to the eye about as much as chlorophyll chewing gum appeals to the mouth.

I backtracked to the Tabernacle and turned into the gravel parking lot. Pines and small oaks border the lot. A beat-up red pickup and the blue Plymouth in which Eunice Gilmore's body was found sat in the dust. The church itself is a squat frame building made up of one medium-sized and one small rectangle. The second is joined to the first at the larger ones back left corner. I suppose the small one was added when the congregation raised sufficient funds to expand. Both sections bear dull white paint.

Most folks who attend services at the Tabernacle farm several acres for a living or work in one of the textile mills in the area. Many of them do both. If you walked up to one of them on the job, you wouldn't guess he says *amen* out loud when the preacher makes a good point on Sunday or speaks in an unknown tongue during Wednesday night's prayer meeting. Over the years I've heard some colorful stories about the church, but I understand it has calmed down quite a bit since the fathers and mothers of the present congregation sat in the pews.

* * * *

You would never see Earl Gilmore sitting at the counter in Mabel's Red Pig. He'd probably prefer egg salad sandwiches. Now that I've talked to him, I'll also have to say that he hardly seems the man to lead the little flock of farmers and mill workers at the Tabernacle. I can't imagine what's kept him there nine years. The man is arrogant. He acts as if he thinks he belongs one step up. Maybe he does. On the other hand, he might belong many, many steps down.

It seemed peculiar knocking at a church door, but I did it this time to avoid startling Earl Gilmore. He opened the wooden door and extended his right hand. "Come in, Lawyer Wilkie," he said without smiling. He wore a white, short-sleeved shirt that was unbuttoned at the collar. He is under six feet tall and at least twenty pounds overweight. His graying black hair is cut too short to be parted in the middle, but that's the way he wears it. Today it stuck up stubbornly near the crown. He has very fair skin, and his face is puffy like an overweight adolescent's. If my memory serves me right, the newspaper reported he's in his early fifties.

I followed him through the large rectangle, which is where preaching services are held. Two rows of modest oak pews lead to the front of the room. There is seating for maybe a hundred and twenty people. When we reached the front, I noted the altar and choir pews are also oak. An upright piano on the right of the choir loft provides music. I suppose my niece Sylvia sat on the black piano bench before Maizie decided the job was too dangerous for her. At the front left corner, Rev. Gilmore opened a door and we entered a small hallway. To the right a cement stairway led downstairs to the basement of the larger building, and on the left the hallway split the middle of the smaller building. The preacher turned left into the hallway. "My office is at the end of this hall," he said. "These other rooms are Sunday School classes."

"After we talk," I said, "I'd like to see the basement where Mrs. Gilmore died."

He hesitated a moment before replying. "All right," he said.

At the end of the hall, we entered a tiny room. A keyhole desk filled its center portion. Beside it sat a tall peach basket turned upside down with a telephone on top of it. He sat down behind the desk on a straight-backed wooden chair and offered me the only other seat, a metal folding chair. Up against the wall at the right of his desk, two orange crates sat on top of each other, posing as a bookcase. I noted a King James Version of the Bible, but no Revised Standard Version, was part of his little library. A couple other titles caught my eye, titles I knew I'd never see in my own church. What use would we Presbyterians have for *Introducing Children to the Holy Ghost*? or *Symbolic Interpretation of Unknown Tongues*?

Reverend Gilmore sat staring at me. "What is it I can do for you, Lawyer?" he asked. His icy blue eyes made me wish I had written down my questions in advance.

I told him I appreciated his giving me his time and that I had been hired to represent Buck Eudy if or when the case came to trial.

"What do you mean *if or when*?" he said. "There has been a murder. Buck has been accused. There will be a trial."

His statements sounded like three points in a Sunday sermon.

"I honestly believe Buck to be innocent of the murder, Rev. Gilmore. Do you know both Archie and Red Byerly were present at the scene of the crime the night your wife died?"

"The Byerlys might have had opportunity to commit the murder," he said, "but neither had motive. Buck Eudy did. He threw a fit when my wife demanded he do the job this church was paying him to. The ball team heard the argument and he became embarrassed. I didn't approve of my wife's wanting to hire a man who lost one job because he couldn't control his temper in a high school classroom. Her decision remained a source of contention between us during the last months of her life. Giving him responsibilities in our church was

203

putting our young people at risk. It turned out that her decision to hire him also put her at risk, dire risk." His eyes were dry. His voice did not waver. The man has preached dozens of funerals and counseled twice as many grieving relatives. I suppose his experiences serve him well in controlling his own grief.

"Still, I plan to question the Byerlys," I said. "I think Sheriff Shepherd might have acted too hastily in bringing the accusation against Buck."

"He found several of Buck's prints on the handle of that big push broom. Buck came back after the party broke up. He and my wife may have quarreled a second time. At any rate, he dealt her several blows with the broom. He'd probably wanted to hit her in precisely the same way when she delivered her lecture to him in front of the group of young people."

"The sheriff said only one print was clear," I said. "The others were smudged. Someone, obviously the murderer, wiped off part of the handle. Of course, it could have been Buck, but it could also have been someone else. Someone who wanted to clean off his own prints while leaving several of Buck's. I also find it noteworthy that no trace of Buck's prints showed up on your Plymouth. Only your wife's and yours."

He locked eyes with me. His expression reminded me of a man on the witness stand who suddenly realizes my questions to him have kept his testimony from adding up properly.

"You must intend to leave no stone unturned in your defense of this man." His voice held no emotion.

"Will you answer a few questions that, I admit, sound like I'm prying into your personal life, Reverend Gilmore?"

"That depends, Lawyer Wilkie. Why don't you ask one and then I'll know how personal you plan to be."

"I understand uncomplimentary drawings of Mrs. Gilmore appeared on a church wall a month or so ago. Is that correct?"

"Yes, that's right," he said and gave me an indulgent look. "Do you have children, Lawyer Wilkie?"

"A niece who used to play for choir practice here at your church and three nephews, but no children of my own, I'm afraid." I always try to manage a smile when someone asks me this question.

He gave a nod. "Well then, you may not know how common it is for young folks to resent any sort of authority. My wife was morally upright and asked that all our young people be the same. I'm afraid some found righteousness a hard pill to swallow."

"And did your own children resent her guidance?" I asked, knowing the answer he'd have to give.

He colored and paused before answering. "No," he said, "we have no children of our own."

"More than one member of your church has said Mrs. Gilmore was particularly hard to get along with these past few months. Being her husband, you would, of course, be the first to have noticed this change in her." I waited for him to react.

"I have no idea what you mean. My wife was always a strong-willed woman."

Allowing Jaybird Blanton to remain anonymous, I retold his story about Mrs. Gilmore's thwarting the plan for a fish fry. The Reverend frowned as I talked.

"Yes," he responded when I finished. "I remember when those men had to give up their plans. Hubie Fort, our unofficial chef, told me how disappointed they all were. I don't know whether lawyers' wives are like preachers' wives," he continued, "but my wife was often suspicious of my dealings with women in the congregation, or any women, for that matter."

"I've heard of ministers being accused of letting their sexual desires trip them up," I said. "Sometimes it leads to a dismissal even if it is never proved."

"Yes. Eunice and I encountered that problem a couple years after we moved here. A female member of the church sometimes showed up for services with bruises on her face and arms. Her brute of a husband drove an Akers truck, thus was gone for days at a time. Often when he returned home, he accused her of having been with other men and beat her. Finally, Akers fired him for almost killing a man in a truck stop brawl. Life was even harder for the woman until he left her and went to work on a fishing boat over on the coast, I thought it was the best thing that could have happened to this woman."

I nodded my head in agreement.

"She worked at the Leland Hosiery Mill and had only one child, so she was not left desperate. I visited her in her home and talked with her in my office. The rumor spread among my church members—and I believe it originated in the choir—that the two of us were having an affair. It became so unpleasant for the woman—and for me—that she moved her membership to a church on the other side of town. I fault myself for allowing one of the counseling sessions I conducted with her to take place during choir practice and for comforting the woman by putting my arm around her during the session." He crossed his arms and shook his head before continuing. "Female church members do occupy an inordinate amount of my time, but during my twenty-three years as an ordained minister, I have never stepped outside the role of pastor with them."

"So you think that women, not men or children, cause a man in your position the most grief?"

"I wouldn't put it exactly like that." His voice was patient, his eyes steady. "God chose me to care for the people of this congregation. It is my experience that men require less care than women. God made them that way. Children, of course, are easiest to deal with. Their youth makes them as pliable as clay. It's not difficult to mold them into what you know their Maker intended."

"But what a responsibility," I said. "How can a person be certain he knows what God intended?"

"Lawyer Wilkie, you have asked the wrong question. You should have asked how a child can know what God intended unless we adults lead him."

Not wanting to push him too hard, I let his remark lie for a minute. I allowed my eyes to wander again to the book about children and the Holy Ghost in his orange-crate bookcase. "Yes, I see your point," I finally answered. "But it's still a powerful responsibility. Fortunately, church people, school teachers, and parents all pitch in to mold a child. I guess they act as checks and balances on each other."

The sun coming through the room's single window filtered through a Venetian blind and printed light and dark lines on the preacher's face. He remained silent so I continued. "If they could all be trusted to do their parts, we might read fewer accounts of abuse. But not many years ago, I read a magazine article about a Catholic priest accused of things that were totally unpardonable, acts he committed on boys under his care in a school run by his church."

Gilmore flinched slightly.

"He was disciplined by the church, of course, but that didn't save those boys from what they'd suffered and from the damage they will live with the rest of their lives."

The minister lowered his brows and a slow anger simmered in his eyes. He stood and moved past me to the door. It wasn't hard to figure out what was coming next.

"Perhaps in the Presbyterian Church, you read too many secular materials and not enough passages from the Bible, Lawyer." He placed his hand firmly on the doorknob. "Let me show you out now."

As we made our way back toward the main entrance, we passed the stairs to the basement. I knew I wasn't going to get to inspect the murder scene today, nor was I going to spring the day camp story on him. That was okay. Sheriff Tubby Shepherd had inspected the basement, and he would appreciate discussing the day camp story much more than this angry preacher would.

* * * *

As I stepped back out into the sunlight, I felt like something dark and heavy lifted off me. Without looking back, I made my way across the parking lot to my Buick. At the edge of the lot A tall, heavyset, red-haired boy pulled a metal trash can along, picking up papers and small tree limbs. Recognizing Red Byerly, I took a few steps toward him and then bent to get a brown paper bag he'd missed. Like some high school boy, I wadded it into a ball and aimed for the trash can.

"Basket," he said as my bag hit the rim and bounced in.

"I'm Clayton Wilkie," I said and put out my hand.

"Red Byerly," he answered. His hand was as big as mine but had fewer wrinkles and no age spots.

"Are you a member here, Mr. Byerly?" I asked.

"No, I never joined up, but I do go to services from time to time. I work for Reverend Gilmore. He hired me to do the job Buck Eudy used to do round here."

A noise came from the front of the church building and we both looked in its direction. Earl Gilmore stood framed by the open church door. "Red, it's quitting time," he said. "Your pay stopped ten minutes ago. I'll expect you back day after tomorrow at ten sharp." He turned abruptly and shut the door with a bang.

Red drew in a deep breath and blew it out through closed lips. "That man can shore keep you guessing," he said. "Yesterday, I left ten minutes early and he blew his top."

"I've been hired to represent Buck Eudy in the murder case that's coming up, Mr. Byerly."

"I'm Red, Lawyer Wilkie. I know you're Buck's lawyer. Sheriff Shepherd told me when he questioned me last week."

"Well, Red, I'd like to buy you a cup of coffee or a Pepsi and ask you a few questions myself. You ever go to Mabel's Red Pig?"

"From time to time."

"Maybe you'd like a barbecue sandwich with your drink."

"Sounds good. The sheriff told me you'd get a copy of my dep—dep— what is it they call it?"

"Deposition."

"Yeah, that's it. He said you'd probably be wanting to ask me some questions and that I should cooperate. Tell you what. I'll follow you in my truck. Then I can go on to a paint job I'm working on over at the armory."

* * * *

If Mabel wondered what I was doing back at the Pig just two hours after I had my barbecue with Emerson, she gave no indication. I asked questions for thirty minutes while Red ate his barbecue and we both drank Pepsis. The information I got from him agreed with what he had told the sheriff. The night of the murder he hung around Black

Bottom drinking beers until around 11 PM but talked to no one. His alibi might as well be non existent. If anyone saw him there, I doubt they would come forward. Over the years the people living down there have learned that life goes better for them if they remain unseen and unheard. Sometimes, I think they're right. It's a shame but it's the truth.

He said he ran out of beer around 11 PM and drove to the church where Mrs. Gilmore had allowed him to sleep these past months. He saw a patrol car in the church parking lot and feared he might be blamed for whatever was wrong. He drove by, parked down the road, and hid in the woods that rim the edge of the parking lot. After watching for a while, he left quietly and spent three days hiding near Black Bottom. Last week Sheriff Shepherd informed me that he and his deputy had seen no sign of Red at the crime scene on Thursday night. Neither had they seen Red's father there.

"It was Mrs. Gilmore, not her husband, who took you in originally, wasn't it?" I asked.

"That's right, Lawyer. Before that, I bought beer and liquor with every penny I got my hands on."

"While she was alive, you helped out at the church as a volunteer, didn't you?"

"Yeah, it's the least I could do. I was getting my bed free, and she usually brought me a meal each day. Some people thought Mrs. Gilmore was cold, but she had a streak most people didn't see. She never had no kids of her own and she might've been overbearing if she had. But she was good to me."

"It could be because you're not a kid. You're almost grown. That, and the fact that you were new to her. You hadn't grown up in her house and caused her a thousand small problems."

Red's face took on a puzzled expression.

"My wife and I are childless like the Gilmores," I continued. "We always had great patience when we tended to our niece so that her parents could leave Harmony for a weekend. On the other hand, they often became frustrated with daily behavior they deemed improper. You see what I'm getting at?"

"Yeah, I guess so. My mama didn't have a whole lot of patience with me when she was alive, and my old man don't know the meaning of the word. I'll be the first to admit, though, that I raised some hell for them."

"How did you come to be a paid caretaker at the church?"

"After I came out of hiding and talked to Sheriff Shepherd, I went by the Tabernacle to pick up my clothes. I figured I'd have to move back in with my old man. The Preacher surprised me in the basement and struck up a conversation. I asked him if he needed a janitor now that Buck was in jail. He'd never paid me much attention before, but he thought about it awhile and said he'd give me a try."

"What do you mean he hadn't paid you much attention?"

Red lowered his head slightly and shook it. Then he met my eyes and answered. "Fact is, he gave me as much attention as I wanted him to, which was none. There's stories that go round about him. You probably never heard them."

"What kind of stories?"

212

"Well, there's two kinds," he answered. "I've heard talk of him hugging and kissing women who come crying to him when their husbands leave them.. I don't put much stock in them stories though."

"And what's the other kind?"

He looked me straight in the eye. "Some people wonder why the Tabernacle always has summer camp for little boys but never for little girls."

"Is that right?"

"Long time ago when I was little myself," he continued, "I begged to go to that camp. I heard they had a lake you could swim in and a ball field and plenty of hot dogs. Sounded good to me, but my mama near about had a cow when I asked her to let me go. She told me the farther away I stayed from that holy-roller preacher, the better off I'd be."

"But now you work for him?"

"Yeah." He forced a short laugh. "With my reputation, who else in this town is going to give me a job? The paintin' I do here and there won't put gas in my truck and keep me fed. And remember, I get to sleep free of charge on a cot in the Tabernacle's basement. Besides, I've heard the Reverend prefers little boys. Nobody I know would call me little."

We both laughed and he wiped grease off his mouth with the back of his hand.

"Thanks for the barbecue," he said. "Good luck with your case, but you got one hard row to hoe if you plan to get Buck Eudy off."

"Much obliged for your time, Red," I replied. "Let me know if anything else occurs to you."

He looked down and thumped his finger against his empty drink bottle. Then he raised his eyes and said, "Will do," and headed for the door.

Chapter 18

Sins of the Father

After Lawyer Wilkie left my school, people who'd seen him get me out of class kept asking me who he was and what he wanted. I'm not used to being the center of attention, but I'll have to admit I liked it. It sure kept me from moping around and having second thoughts about breaking up with Luke.

When I got home from school, I barely had time to make me a peanut butter cracker before I heard Sonny's bicycle throwing gravel in our driveway. I put ice cubes into glasses and poured us some Pepsi. Mama and Daddy don't allow Linda Sue and me to have any company inside the house until they get home from work, so we sat down on the breezeway steps. Linda Sue showed up for just long enough to make a couple smart remarks and then went back in to work on her homework. Sonny listened without a word while I told him I'd talked to Clayton Wilkie and that he was going to report the things I'd seen at the day camp to Sheriff Shepherd. "So," I ended, "I guess I've done about all I can to help solve this murder and get Buck out of jail."

He tilted his head to one side and said "Don't be so sure of that. Have you actually been to the crime scene since the murder?"

"No, not except for going with Luke to Mrs. Gilmore's funeral," I answered. "Why?"

"We need to get out to the Tabernacle so we can go over the basement where Mrs. Gilmore died. And it wouldn't hurt to do a little spying on the preacher."

I laughed out loud. "You want to help Buck or you want to play Sgt. Joe Friday?" I asked.

"Nothing says we can't do both." He grinned. "And we need to get with Red Byerly again. Something tells me he knows more than he's telling."

I smiled. "You still jealous because I got to question Red on Easter Sunday while you sat home doing a biology project?"

"No, you did okay that time, but remember he's working for Gilmore every day and sleeping in the Tabernacle's basement. We don't know how much he's seen out there since you talked to him. You think you can get your daddy's wheels for a little while?"

216

"No, not to spy on the preacher." I frowned and thought for a minute. "How'd you like to do an errand for my mama? Linda Sue's birthday's coming up in a week, and Mama told me yesterday she wants me to go over to Mrs. Nell Sides' house and get her to bake us a lemon pound cake with birthday icing. Mrs. Nell needs all the orders she can get now that Cleg's lost another job."

Sonny shook his head and then stared off into space. "My mama says he's as trifling as my own daddy," he said. "He left us ten years ago to find out if money was growing on trees out in Texas."

"Maybe it's a blessing that Mrs. Nell and Cleg never had any kids," I said. His brown eyes moved back to mine, and the corners of his mouth turned up into a little smile that was not much different from a frown.

About that time the Chevy rolled down the driveway, and I got to Mama before she could crawl out. She agreed that this was a good time to let Mrs. Nell know what we needed, and I asked her to tell Linda Sue something or other so she wouldn't want to tag along with Sonny and me.

Daddy got out and brushed the lint off his overalls. He handed me the keys and looked at me like he knew we had more than a birthday cake on our minds. "You be careful," he said.

Before Daddy could change his mind, Sonny and I hopped into the car and drove the half block to the Calloways' house. His sister Jane had dropped her schoolbooks on their front porch where she was sitting on the steps playing jack rocks. I borrowed a sheet of paper and a pencil from her. While Sonny told his mama where we were going, I wrote out a note to Mrs. Nell telling her all about the birthday cake and even drawing a picture of the kid with a yellow pony tail I wanted on the top. Ten minutes later we had slipped it into the black metal mailbox on Mrs. Nell's front porch and were on our way to the Deliverance Tabernacle.

The only sign of life around the building was Red Byerly's old pickup parked under a scrawny tree. "Hot dog! We're in luck," Sonny said. "Preacher ain't here."

We pulled up beside the pickup and crossed the parking lot to the church. Three wooden steps took us off the red clay and up to a porch half the size of a school blackboard. Sonny balled up his hand into a fist and banged on the door. In a minute, we heard noises inside and Red opened the door.

He was surprised to see us. "What you want?" he asked.

Sonny moved a couple inches closer to Red. Beside Sonny, who is not much taller than me, Red looked every inch of his six feet. I doubt that many people would care to take him on in a fight. In his best Sgt. Friday voice, Sonny said, "Red, me and Jonnie got reason to believe you could be accused of murder in the near future. Open up this door and we'll tell you what we know."

I could almost hear the *Dragnet* theme song: "Dum-de-dum-dum."

Red's eyes got big and he stuttered something. He looked all around the parking lot before he opened the door to let us in. "Wh— What you mean accused of murder?" he asked.

218

"Calm down, Red." I gave Joe Friday a hateful look. "Truth is, we just needed a way to get in here and snoop around a little. Where's Rev. Gilmore?"

"Out visiting the sick and the old people. Just left." Red twisted a dust rag round and round in his big hands and looked toward the door we'd just come through like he thought the preacher might've changed his mind and come back. "You ain't heard nothing new from the sheriff, have you?" he asked.

"No, but Buck's lawyer thinks several people besides Buck look suspicious for one reason or another. He did mention your name, Red."

Red's eyes jerked to the entry door again and then toward the front of the assembly room. A door up there to the left of the choir loft opens to a little hallway. If you turn left in the hall, you're in the building that houses the Sunday School classes and Rev. Gilmore's office. If you turn right in the hall, you're on the basement stairs. "Why don't we go down to the basement to talk?" Red said. "C'mon, that's where I sleep." So that's how Sonny and me got to poke around at the very scene of the murder. Or at least, we thought we were going to poke around.

We stopped at the bottom of the stairs, where a large push broom leaned against the black iron handrail. As I put my hand out and rubbed its smooth handle, I realized the new hadn't worn off it yet. It must've been the replacement for the one the murderer used on Mrs. Gilmore.

"Where's your bed?" Sonny asked.

219

"My cot's behind that." Red pointed to a large folding screen on our right. Somebody had built it out of plywood but never bothered to paint it.

"You mean you sleep up under the stairs?" Sonny said.

Red frowned. "No, that's where they store cleaning equipment and other stuff. The screen's supposed to hide all that and my cot too, but it ain't big enough for the job."

Luke and I'd been to dinners in the basement, but I'd never had any reason to look behind the screen. I took a few steps and peeked behind it. Red saw me eyeing his sleeping quarters and added, "Lots of cardboard boxes back there too. Some of that stuff, they ought to go on and throw out. Them ragged hymn books, for instance."

Sonny started toward the screen, but Red blocked him and said, "We ain't here to take no tour. Come on." I wanted to see more of the sleeping area and to look for blood on those cement steps, but Red was worried about being accused of a murder. He led us toward the middle of the room.

The place looks like any other church basement made up of just one big room. The walls are gray cement blocks, and the floors are covered with dark gray linoleum. Five or six wooden tables stand in the middle. More are folded up and stacked against the right wall. Somebody painted them a dull green with paint he must've found at the army surplus store you pass a mile before you get to the Tabernacle. Gray metal chairs covered with scratch marks and rust are pushed up under the tables. A metal sink, a Frigadaire, and a stove

220

line up on the wall opposite the stair wall. Wooden shelves over the sink hold cooking pans, paper plates, Wesson oil—things like that. Casserole dishes and Tupperware bowls church women have left behind fill one of the shelves. It's the same at my church.

Red set us down at the first table we reached. He sat across from us. I told him he shouldn't get too worked up over Sonny's warning. Some of his daddy's and the preacher's actions seemed just as suspicious as his own. When I mentioned Archie, Red let his head fall like he was looking at his chest. I wondered if I'd gone too far. Even if he didn't get along with his daddy and called him "my old man," that didn't necessarily mean he wanted him accused of murder. Nothing came to my mind to say next, so we all three just sat there for what seemed like a long time. Every once in a while, the old church building above us would creak. It was more than a little bit spooky.

Finally, Red looked up. His eyes were wet. "Jonnie," he said, "I been lying about that Thursday night Mrs. Gilmore died."

My mouth dropped open and I sucked in air.

"Are you for real?" Sonny whispered.

"I told you and everybody else I left that softball cookout early and drank beer down by the railroad tracks in Black Bottom till eleven o'clock."

"That's what you said to me in your daddy's barn on Easter Sunday," I agreed.

"Well it's not the truth," he said. "Least not the whole truth."

"You need to give us the facts," Sonny chimed in. I shot him another hard look.

221

"I ain't told the honest truth so far 'cause I don't like what I know and I ain't sure what I'm going to do with it." He looked down at the green tabletop like he hoped to find the answer to his problem scratched in the dull paint.

"Is it something that might help the sheriff find Mrs. Gilmore's real killer?" I asked.

He raised his eyes. "The sheriff's got Buck in jail already. Changing my story might put the spotlight on me. Besides, I lied the first time; the sheriff might think I'm lying again."

I felt uneasy hearing Red admit he'd been lying—real uneasy. But at the same time, I was dying to know what he'd failed to tell. "If you want to give it a spin right now with nobody to hear but Sonny and me, that might help you get things straight in your mind," I said.

"I'm gonna tell you," he said. I've 'bout decided not to kill the preacher, after all. My old man neither."

If he had said he'd decided not to kill Sonny and me, I wouldn't have been any more shocked. It was my turn to stutter. "Not—Not kill the preacher?" I managed to get out. As far as I was concerned, his daddy wouldn't be much of a loss to the world.

"Reckon I'll start at the beginning." He covered his mouth with his big hand for a minute before going on. "I did get bored and leave that cookout early," he said. "I drove around awhile looking at the scenery. You know. White girls sitting out on their front porches after supper, a couple Black Bottom girls standing on the corner in tight shorts. I was just killing time, waiting for everybody to clear out over at the church."

"So you didn't fall off the wagon after all?" What I really wanted to know was why he'd been thinking of killing Rev. Gilmore. I hoped he'd get back to that in his own good time.

"No, not right then anyway."

"What did you do next?" Sonny asked.

"I gave up and went back to the church to go to bed. I musta got back to the Tabernacle at nine o'clock or shortly thereafter. Mrs. Gilmore's car was the only one left in the parking lot."

"If I'm not mistaken, your daddy told my daddy and George Eudy he'd gone looking for you at the Tabernacle that night around nine or ten o'clock. He wanted to collect past rent and board from you out of the money Humpy Barrier had paid you to help him paint his house. But he said the church was dark and nobody was around."

"He was lying. I know he was and I know why he was too."

"My daddy said he might've been trying to give you an alibi."

Red looked at me like I'd just told him a joke that wasn't very funny. "Wrong. You ain't nowhere close to the truth. It's not me, it's hisself he's trying to save."

Sonny had been rared back in his chair listening. He sat straight up. The front legs of his chair hit the floor with a clank. "Do you mean your daddy killed Mrs. Gilmore?" he asked. His words bounced off the basement's cement-block walls. They irritated Red.

"I don't know exactly what I mean, Calloway." Red pooched out his lower lip and thought for a minute. "Tell you what. Why don't you just let me finish telling what I started? Okay?"

223

A creak sounded above us and we all raised our eyes toward the ceiling.

"It's this building," Red said. "The members built it theirselves, and it ain't worth the nails they used to put it up. You ought to try sleeping down here at night."

I hoped Sonny would hold his tongue. Not knowing why Red had wanted to kill the preacher made me wonder if we'd made a mistake coming down here alone with him.

"So, like I said, 'bout nine o'clock I was back at the church," he continued. "I came in through the main door and made my way toward the front of the assembly room so I could go down the basement stairs. But when I opened the door to the little hall, I heard my old man's fat mouth. I figured he was drunk and he had to be talking to Mrs. Gilmore. I tiptoed down the hall to the preacher's office. The ruckus was coming from there, so I just stood real quiet outside the door and listened."

"Was he mad at her for taking you in?" I asked

"Oh yeah. But there's more to it than that. A whole lot more. My old man's a rotten bastard," he said. "You don't know how rotten, not yet anyhow."

Red was breathing heavy. He sat there for a minute clinching and unclenching his big fists on the table top. Finally he said, "Mrs. Gilmore told him I didn't live under his roof any more and he had no claim on any money I earned now. Well, that really set him on fire. He started banging around inside the office. He knocked over the preacher's peach basket and the phone that sits on top it. I moved into the room across the hall so I could see what was going on better. I stood against the wall behind its open door and looked through the crack. At first, I was scared he was trying to hurt Mrs. Gilmore, but he was just stumbling around drunk. He got right up in her face and put both hands on her shoulders and said, 'Now you just set here in the preacher's chair and listen to me, Missus. I'm goin' to tell you somethin' about bein' piss poor. You goin' find out how people in poor families have to help each other when it comes to money.'

"I thought he intended on giving her the same rigmarole he always gives me when he wants my money, but he came out with something I'd never heard before."

I glanced at Sonny. His brown eyes were big as paddle balls.

Red put one of his fists up to his mouth and bit on his knuckle. He stared down at the table. I was afraid he'd changed his mind about telling the story, but after a while he raised his eyes and looked across at me. "Jonnie, this is hard to say in front of a girl. But I guess if I can get it out to you, I won't have no trouble at all in front of the sheriff."

I swallowed and nodded.

"My old man started out standing beside her chair looking down at her while he talked. He said, 'Hell yeah, my boy's got to make money to help me out.'"

I was surprised at how much Red sounded like Archie. Maybe it was easier for him to let the awful things come out in Archie's voice than to tell them himself. Still, the gravely voice made me feel creepy. Red went on.

"He claimed people in Harmony wouldn't give him enough work to get by on. He talked about being in the middle of painting a man's house one time and missing a couple days 'cause he was sick. Said the man up and fired him." Red looked across the table at me. "He wasn't sick," he said. "He was drunk. That kind of thing happened all the time."

"What was Mrs. Gilmore doing while he talked?" Sonny asked.

"She tried to interrupt him," Red said, "but he didn't give her much of a chance. If you've ever tried talking to a drunk, you know what I mean." Red looked down at his fists on the table. "The rest of what came out of that sorry drunk's mouth ain't fit for anybody to hear," he said without looking up.

I leaned in toward him. "Go on, Red," I whispered.

"He said people were dead set on keeping him from earning a decent living, so he had to turn to my mama to bring in extra money. I'll never forget his stinking words."

Red's eyes narrowed and he took on Archie's voice again. "'Rose had always took in ironin'. Worked like some nigger woman, but what she brought in didn't come nowhere close to what we needed to get by. The time came when I had to make her sell the thing women have sold since before the time of Jesus, I reckon.'"

His words hit me like the sight of a dirty rubber Linda Sue and I found one morning on our way to school. Sonny looked like he was in a state of shock too.

Red shook his head. "I couldn't believe what he was saying—and to Mrs. Gilmore, of all people. The look on her face woulda stopped any sober human, but not my old man. No sir, he went right on. He said years ago when Mama was alive, Rev. Gilmore had come to our door willing to pay for her services. He said if you took all the times together that Mama had actually satisfied the preacher, you wouldn't come up with enough spit to fill a Dixie cup. Said he didn't know what the preacher was trying to prove, but according to Mama, he'd usually end up sniveling about his little boys being the only ones loved him."

"His little boys?" I asked. Red didn't know the tale I knew about the day camp, but this was sure no time for me to butt in and tell it.

"I ain't sure just what he meant by that," Red said, "but I got a pretty good guess. Anyway, that's not where I'm headed right now.

"I felt like busting into that office and killing my old man with my bare hands for selling my mama like that. His drinking was what had put us in the shape we was in. I used to see him come home from painting and go into Mama's sewing box to take money she'd put away from her ironing. Then he'd buy him a pint of liquor and not go to the job until twelve noon the next day—if he went at all. It got to the place where people wouldn't hire him."

"But you didn't kill him," I said.

"I couldn't. Not with Mrs. Gilmore there. It woulda flew in the face of all she'd tried to teach me. But I ain't gonna deny I *felt* like killing him and the preacher too. They both used my mama like she was dirt."

Red's fists were clinched so tight that his knuckles had turned white. "But she wasn't dirt," he said. "She'd a-made ten of either one of them." He wrinkled up his forehead and looked back down at the table for a long time before he raised his eyes and said, "This ain't nothing to be putting out in front of a girl, Jonnie. Maybe I need to go ahead and call the sheriff."

"Don't worry about me," I said. "I know you're not telling this story to embarrass me." Truth be told, I think Red was the one who was embarrassed. After all, he was talking about his own mama. I looked him straight in the eye and said, "You're trying to right a wrong, Red. Go ahead."

"All right," he answered. "I could tell Mrs. Gilmore was scared bad. Most times she was a woman who could keep her cool, but she was wringing her hands. My old man stumbled over to the preacher's desk and plopped his no good butt down on it right beside the Holy Bible. He went at her about nobody, and especially not her, having any call to try to take me away from him. Then he pulled the ace out from up his sleeve.

"As close as I can remember, his words were: 'You better watch yourself, Missus. Your so-called husband tried to get somethin' for nothin' out of my family five years ago. He knew I 'uz the one to go through if he wanted Rose's services. But he sweet talked her into goin' to Black Bottom with him one Friday night when I weren't home. One of my buddies come into Hub's Cafe that night. He said

228

the preacher and Rose had bothered him out in the woods when he 'uz tryin' to do some serious drinkin'. So I went home to get my pistol an' then I went to Black Bottom myself. Found 'em buck naked, rootin' around in the dirt not forty yards from the railroad tracks. That preacher's a pitiful excuse of a man. I guess you know that already, Missus.'"

I wanted to put my arm around Red's shoulder. His sad eyes met mine for a minute. "Jonnie, I know this is awful and I'm sorry," he said and then went on.

"My old man said, 'The two of 'em 'uz goin' at it so hard they didn't see me till I 'uz right at 'em. The preacher rolled off Rose so I shot her first. Meant to get him too but the trigger dropped on a damn empty chamber.'

"Then he blamed me for causing him to run out of bullets," Red said. The bastard told Mrs. Gilmore I was no count. That I'd used his pistol to shoot rabbits for supper but then forgot to reload it. When he got back to his story, he said the gunshot made the preacher pull up his pants and run. He tried to go after him and kill him some way or other, but he tripped on a tree root and hit the ground so hard he was out cold for an hour or so." Red stopped talking. He breathed little short breaths for a minute and then started again.

"Mrs. Gilmore looked like she was about to have a stroke. She tried to say something, but he warned her to hush till he got through. I wanted to go in and knock his teeth down his filthy throat, but something made me let him keep talking. I felt like I was in a picture show watching something that was too awful to be true.

229

"He told Mrs. Gilmore that when he saw the blood on Mama's chest, he knew he better hightail it out-a there. The next day, he called the sheriff and said he'd been out drinking the night before and couldn't find his wife when he got home. The sheriff didn't do much searching though. A colored man come up on her body two weeks later when he was out looking his rabbit boxes." Red stopped again like he'd forgotten the rest of the story. I prayed Sonny wouldn't ask a question before he finished.

"The Law investigated Mama's death," Red said. "They asked my old man a ton of questions, but they couldn't pin it on him. He'd thrown the gun into Rhino Creek, and the evidence at the murder scene told them a male other than Archie Byerly was having his way with Rose Byerly that night. The questions scared my old man so bad he decided not to kill the preacher like he'd intended. He knew Gilmore would keep his mouth shut, couldn't afford to do nothing else. As far as punishing the preacher, he figured the man was probably walking around in a Hell on Earth after that scene at Black Bottom. Thought that'd be punishment enough."

Red raised his eyes from the table but didn't look directly at either of us. "Now you know my real story and my mama's too," he said. "My old man got tired of rantin' and left the church. Mrs. Gilmore picked up the phone like she was fixing to make a call. I didn't know what I was going to do. I needed time to figure things out, so I snuck out of the church. I didn't go to Black Bottom like I told everybody, though. Back when I'd went on the wagon, I'd hid me a couple bottles of Schlitz in the stone urn in front of my mama's tombstone and four more under rocks nearby. I drove to the cemetery and fished them out. Downed half of them in ten minutes. I kept thinking about what them two had put Mama through. I mean to tell you, I was low. I even asked her there at the grave what I could do to make things right. That's when I decided I'd kill that son-of-a-bitch preacher."

"So that's why you wanted Buck's old job. It'd give you a chance to get Gilmore," Sonny said.

"Yeah. But I needed a place to sleep too. No way I was going back to my old man's place. He killed my mama."

"But you decided not to kill your daddy?" Sonny said.

"Tell you the truth, Calloway, I've give it enough thought now to know I ain't gonna kill either one of 'em."

I let out a long breath and smiled at Red.

He looked back and forth from me to Sonny. "Both of you go to church," he went on. "You learned all the stuff Mrs. Gilmore taught me about Jesus going to the cross. I figure I'm already in debt enough to Him without adding to it. Besides, us Byerlys have hung enough rotten stories on our name. If my mama could rise up from her grave, I think she'd tell me enough is enough."

Red's big shoulders had drooped almost as much as his face while he told his sad story. "That's a heavy story to carry around by yourself," I said to him.

"Better give it up to Sheriff Shepherd," Sonny added.

"Yeah, I guess so. 'Specially since they're thinking I might be the one who killed Mrs. Gilmore," Red agreed.

"Who do *you* think killed her?" Sonny asked.

Red pinched his chin between his thumb and forefinger. "Well, it sure wasn't me," he said. "And before he left the church, I heard my old man say he meant no harm to her as long as she left me alone and kept her mouth shut about him shooting my mama."

"So that leaves?" said Sonny.

Red didn't hesitate for a minute. "Buck Eudy."

"Or the Reverend Earl T. Gilmore," I added.

None of us heard the footsteps on the basement stairs.

Chapter 19

A Harmony Whodunit

Jonnie's day camp story festered in my mind. My 2 PM meeting with Rev. Gilmore and my talk with Red Byerly at the Pig added to my concern. When Irene Reid allowed me into Tubby's office at 4 PM, I briefed him on what Jonnie Sparks had observed last summer and on Gilmore's reaction to my questions. In ten minutes he and I were on our way to the Sparks home.

He kept his eyes on the road as he moved his brown cruiser through mill traffic. Finally, he spoke. "In the old movies you always suspected the butler. But for the last ten or fifteen years, you wouldn't go bad wrong if you pointed your finger at the jealous husband."

I laughed. "You like those whodunits as much as I like my barbecue."

"Yeah, you might say I'm addicted." His laugh was short, little more than a grunt. "But Harmony's not Hollywood, so I don't let myself get carried away by something I saw Humphrey Bogart do on the movie screen."

"But still, some jealous husbands do kill the one who wronged them," I said. "You don't read about it in *The Telegram*, but you sure do in *The Charlotte Observer*."

"You're right there," he said. "And the way Charlotte's spreading toward Harmony, some of its violence is bound to rub off on us."

"Of course, in this case you can't call Rev. Gilmore a jealous husband," I went on. "If there's any truth to the story about his wife finding him cavorting with the naked boys, I'd say *she* had more reason to get rid of *him* than vice versa."

"Unless she threatened to expose him to his congregation," Tubby said. "If she did and he knew he was guilty of as much or even more than what she accused him, he might've decided he had to put her out of the picture."

"That's a possibility I could buy," I answered. I glanced over at Tubby's speedometer. We were running 45 in a 25 zone.

"I spent a lot of time these past two weeks investigating Archie Byerly and his son Red," he continued, "but I never seriously considered Earl Gilmore."

I nodded my head but didn't answer. In my own career I've guessed wrong about enough cases to understand when a man needs to defend a faulty decision.

"After all," he continued, "Gilmore preaches from a pulpit every Sunday, not to mention conducting weddings and funerals." The sheriff ran a red light.

"Besides, those softball players agreed that Mrs. Gilmore raked Buck Eudy over the coals in front of them that very night," he went on. "It wasn't hard to see him sneaking back after the party broke up and hitting her with the broom the boys said he'd slammed down. The man's lack of self control has been a trademark for him, even when he was a teacher."

"You told me earlier that somebody had attempted to wipe prints off the broom handle," I said.

"That's right but partial prints matching Buck's were still visible. I figured he came back later and the argument continued. He lost his temper and hit her with the broom. When he realized she was dead, he tried to wipe the handle clean but was unsuccessful."

"And you found no significant prints elsewhere."

"Right. Whoever killed her, dragged her body across the basement to the side door near the kitchen. There were minor bloodstains on the linoleum and countless smudged prints on the doorknob. It's a church, you know. Twenty youngsters left prints all over the basement during the softball party that night. The Plymouth's trunk had been wiped clean."

Tubby braked hard and turned into the Sparks' driveway. Lois stuck her head out the screen door. "John's down there working on his plant beds," she said, nodding toward what would be her husband's garden in another month or two. "Hope nothin's wrong."

"No, Mrs. Sparks," Tubby answered. "We just want to get a few more details from your daughter Jonnie. Is she home?" He took a couple steps toward the porch.

Worry lines creased Lois's forehead. "No she's not. Her and Sonny Calloway, from up the street, went off in the car to do something for me." She lowered her voice. "I sent them to see about ordering a birthday cake for Linda Sue, but it shouldn't have taken them over twenty minutes. I don't know where in the world they are now. We ate supper without her."

The screen door flew wide open, and Linda Sue stepped out with her hands on her hips. "I can tell you." She spit out the words. "They're where they got no business being. They went to snoop around over at the Tabernacle."

"Are you sure, Linda Sue?" Lois asked.

"One hundred percent," she said. "I heard them cooking up the idea, but didn't tell on them because I knew I'd at least get a birthday cake out of it."

John Sparks came around the corner of his house, and Tubby hurried to explain why we were there and where Jonnie was. John pulled off his dirty work gloves and started for the sheriff's car. "We better get over there," he said.

Chapter 20

A Clean Sweep

"Well, Little Miss Sparks. My wife used to say you were too smart for your own good. Maybe that was one time she knew what she was talking about." Rev. Gilmore's voice sounded as cold as it did when he calmed down Archie and the pack of dogs at Mrs. Gilmore's funeral.

Red, Sonny, and I stared across the room and up the stairs at him. He stopped before he got all the way to the basement floor and then crossed his arms over his chest and spoke again. "For the most part, however, she was a featherbrain. She could sing, I'll grant you that. However, she wasn't content directing the choir. She wanted

237

people to believe she knew as much about leading a congregation as I do, but most of the time she didn't know which end was up."

The three of us were scared stiff. We sat there like statues while the preacher talked. His voice was louder than it needed to be, loud like he talked when he was up in the pulpit preaching.

"She had trouble following even the simplest of my directions," he said. He came down a couple more steps real slow. His face looked like he might be trying to figure something out.

"I could tell her plainly where to find some item I needed, but nine times out of ten, I'd end up having to locate it myself." Another step.

"Before she left home the night of the softball cookout, I instructed her to bring me a folder from my sermon files here in the basement." He stopped on the bottom step and pointed to a metal filing cabinet against the left wall.

"I wanted to incorporate a quotation from an old sermon into a new one I was working on, so I waited and waited for her to get home. I phoned her twice but got a busy signal both times. Finally, I decided to walk the half mile over here to get the material myself.

"Do you know where I found her?" he asked.

Nobody answered his question. His feet hit the linoleum floor and started across the room toward our table. Suddenly, I had to pee.

He stopped dead still and asked his question again. "Do you know where she had searched for my old sermon?" His voice echoed off the basement walls.

I put one hand on my stomach and held my breath.

He frowned across the room at us and answered his own question. "She was upstairs where I keep only current material. Like I said, half the time the woman didn't know which end was up." He shrugged his shoulders.

The woman had a name. I wondered if he ever called his wife Eunice.

Rev. Gilmore took a couple more steps before he looked at Red and said, "The moment I walked into my office, she began blabbing about your father coming in here drunk looking for you. I told her to shut up about the Byerlys until I did what I'd come to do, and that was to locate a sermon I'd sent her to get. I marched her down those stairs and pulled out that file drawer." He pointed to the stairs he'd just come down and to the top drawer of the file cabinet. Then he turned and shook his finger in our direction like he wanted to make sure we understood his point. He said, "I had to show her what any person with normal brain capacity could have located on his own."

On her own, I thought.

He took another step toward our table and shifted his stare toward Red again. "And as you know, Red Byerly, she had been foolish enough to listen to a tale your wretched father wandered in to tell her. What's worse, I tried to explain the truth behind his drunken babbling, but she was willing to take his word over mine. That was a bad mistake and it was one she paid for. By the way, you made the same mistake when you hid behind the door that night and listened to him rant. You might have been all right, however, if you'd kept the story to yourself instead of spilling it to this nosey pair."

Sweat had popped out on Red's and Sonny's faces. I was so scared I felt like I was going to pee in my pants.

"She preached to me that night like she was in a church pulpit instead of a church basement," he said. "She even threatened to reveal your father's lies to my congregation. I laughed in her face. The idea of a servant of God having anything to do with a prostitute. Humph. Who'd ever believe such a tale?"

Red's face flushed. He came to his feet but stopped short of crossing the basement. Just stood there clenching and unclenching his fists.

Sonny was the first of us to speak. "That story about you and Rose Byerly ain't the only one going round," he said. "What about you and your little boys out at Deliverance Day Camp?"

I couldn't believe my ears. He had no business handing Rev. Gilmore that question. Would Sgt. Joe Friday spit in the face of an armed robber? I broke into a coughing fit. Anything to shut him up. But it was too late.

The preacher backed up to the stairs, grabbed the new push broom and was across the room in a flash flailing it at Sonny. Sonny ducked under the table. I scrambled up and ran past the preacher toward the stairs. When I hit the bottom step, I looked back over my shoulder.

Red was running toward his sleeping quarters. He knocked over the screen and started fumbling around in a big cardboard box

240

under his cot. When he raised up, he had a hunk of stone the size of a dinner plate. He turned toward the table where we'd been sitting. The preacher was bent way over prodding at Sonny with the push broom. Red brought the stone up over his head in both his hands. Then he rared back and aimed it at the preacher's behind, which was stuck straight up in the air.

Bulls-eye! Rev. Gilmore let out a sound that might have been an unknown tongue. Then he hit the floor, still holding the broom.

"Jonnie, go call the sheriff," Red shouted.

I started up the stairs again and almost ran flat into the big belly of Sheriff Tubby Shepherd. My daddy and Lawyer Wilkie followed close on his heels.

"There's no reason for that," Sheriff Shepherd said. Passing me, he hurried across the room to the table that was protecting Sonny. He used both hands to wrench the push broom away from the preacher. Then he slammed it down on the basement floor, probably every bit as hard as Buck Eudy had done that Thursday night Mrs. Gilmore was killed. "But Rev. Gilmore," he said, "you have a mighty lot to answer to. Now get away from that table and don't touch the broom again."

The preacher did as he was told.

Sonny crawled out from under the table. All eyes were on him for a minute. I don't think he reminded a soul of Sgt. Joe Friday.

The sheriff asked Daddy and Lawyer Wilkie to drive Red, Sonny, and me to his office so that he could get statements from each of us. Then he informed Rev. Gilmore he was taking him in for questioning concerning the murder of Eunice Faye Gilmore. He put his hand on the preacher's elbow and led him away to the patrol car. Either he didn't have any handcuffs, or he decided the preacher didn't require them. I don't know which, but I do know Sonny was disappointed.

My daddy put one of his arms around my shoulder and the other around Sonny's. I could tell he wanted to say something but he didn't. His words probably caught in his throat.

Chapter 21

Talk About Courage

Yesterday afternoon when I took the day camp story over to Tubby Shepherd's office, it didn't occur to me that I might end up part of a rescue party. I said as much to my wife last night after we finally got to bed. She lay there awhile without answering, but I knew she wasn't asleep. Finally, she said, "Don't let it go to your head, Clayton, and don't sell any of your law books. You're no more fit to replace Perry Mason than I am to replace Our Miss Brooks." A few minutes later I heard her snoring softly.

She was right, of course, but I lay there half the night reviewing the day's events. My friend Tubby had thanked me for being part of his posse—that's the word he used—but what I did yesterday didn't take a whole lot of courage. No, I wasn't the hero, but then neither was the sheriff.

Last night Tubby placed Rev. Earl T. Gilmore behind bars in the county jail. I sat in his office down the hall with the three youngsters while John Sparks went to get supper for them. In twenty minutes he was back with a bag of cheeseburgers and French fries. Linda Sue followed him with chocolate milk-shakes.

Stanly's a small county and Harmony's a small town. We all know each other, if not personally, then from hearsay. Tubby Shepherd and I go way back. We played on rival football teams in high school. He was quarterback for the Stanly Bulldogs and I was fullback for the Harmony Spiders. We both went away to college for a year, but when our country went to war, we enlisted in the Army and wound up in boot camp together at Fort Bragg. In 1918, I survived the Meuse-Argonne Offensive and returned to Harmony with a Bronze Star and a hip that will continue to bother me the rest of my life. That same year, Tubby came home from Ypres with his Bronze Star and hasn't cared a whole lot about leaving since.

I knew he would have no qualms about me sitting in his office while he questioned the youngsters, but I was surprised when he didn't ask John or Linda Sue to leave. He began by asking Jonnie why she and the Calloway boy had decided to go to the Tabernacle that afternoon.

Linda Sue broke in. "Where they had absolutely no business prowling around."

Tubby turned his patient eyes toward her and asked that she state her name. She tilted her chin up and gave him a wide smile. "Sheriff Shepherd, I'm Linda Sue Sparks, and I knew better than to tag along where Jonnie and Sonny—"

Tubby held up his index finger and told her in a gentle voice that he would ask her questions when they seemed called for. He said if she thought she had relevant information at any other time, he wanted her to raise her hand just like she would in school. She opened her mouth to speak again, but her daddy leveled a firm gaze at her and she thought better of whatever she'd wanted to say.

Again, Tubby asked Jonnie why she and Sonny Calloway had gone to the Tabernacle.

"We wanted to see the steps where Mrs. Gilmore was killed," Jonnie said. "It wasn't up to us to investigate the murder, but our curiosity won over our good sense. So we went."

"I see." Tubby made some notes on a tablet and then added, "Now, why don't you just tell me what happened after you got there."

Jonnie told about meeting Red, who had taken them to the basement. Then her story stalled. She kept describing the basement until Tubby reeled her back in and asked that she stick to what had happened and what had been said.. She tried again but found it difficult to complete her sentences. Finally, she looked at Red Byerly. Her eyes were sad as she said, "I'm sorry, Red, but this part of the story belongs to you".

Then that eighteen-year-old boy spoke up to tell a story that would lead to his father's arrest. Talk about courage! I'll give Red Byerly my Bronze Star any day.

His voice broke several times as he explained how his daddy had killed his mother. Once he stopped to wipe his eyes with the back of his hand. I found the handkerchief Maizie's always sure I have in my back pocket and handed it to him. When he finished, Tubby only asked him a few questions before sending a deputy to arrest Archie Byerly.

The Calloway boy insisted he had facts no one else had mentioned; thus he was allowed to talk. He recounted arrogant statements the preacher had made about his wife before we arrived. One sounded a lot like a threat, and they all sounded like he despised her. Eventually, Calloway reached a scene where the preacher was after him with a push broom. His face colored and he allowed Jonnie to take over again.

She described Sonny crawling around under the table to escape the preacher and her running to get help. Every person in the room laughed when she told of Red Byerly downing the preacher with a large well-aimed stone.

Another Bronze Star, I thought.

Tubby held up his index finger for Jonnie to stop and then looked over at Red. "But Red," he said, "how did you know the stone was among your cleaning rags?"

A choking noise came from the boy's throat. "I—I put it there," he said. "It's not a stone; it's a rose."

246

"What kind of rose, Son?"

Red looked down at his shaky hands a minute before he answered. Then he raised his eyes and said, "It's the kind you find on top a tombstone sometimes."

"Why did you put it there in the basement?" said Tubby.

"Cause I thought it ought to be mine. I took it one night when I was drunk. First, I hid it in my old man's barn and later, at the Tabernacle."

"The caretaker out at Harmony Memorial Park reported that somebody vandalized several of the tombstones on the northern edge of the cemetery during the early part of the winter. Is that where your mama's buried?" Tubby asked.

"Yeah," Red mumbled. "Her name was Rose. The stone rose was hers."

"And when you took it off the top of her gravestone, you knocked over other monuments too, didn't you?"

"I guess I did." He put one hand on his forehead and then ran his fingers through his red hair before continuing. "Like I said, I was drunk. I know that don't make it right, but gimmie a chance and I'll pay for every one of them."

Tubby said they could deal with that problem after this murder case was cleared up and then got to his feet like he was dismissing us. But Red wasn't ready to be dismissed.

"There's one more thing about that rose, Sheriff," he said. "Back at the church you bagged it up and labeled it like you mean to keep it for awhile."

"Yes."

"I guess that's okay by me, but when you're through with it, I want it back. It's all I got left of my mama." His voice cracked and he brushed his hand across his face and wiped his nose before he could finish.

Nobody in that room had a word of rebuttal for Red. Probably, nobody in Harmony would either.

Tubby told Jonnie, Sonny, and Red he wanted to talk to them again in a day or so after he'd done some serious questioning of Earl Gilmore. He thanked Jonnie for her information about the day camp and said he planned to question Luke Goodman about things he might have witnessed going on out there.

His mention of the Goodman boy reminded me I'd failed to tell Tubby about the second piece of information Jonnie had given me. I had little doubt that JB Blanton was responsible for the drawings on the Tabernacle's back wall, but that news was no longer as important as it had been four hours ago. Now that I knew for sure JB was not the person who murdered Mrs. Gilmore, I decided not to share the story with Tubby after all. Maybe the boy's father is the person I need to talk to. Jaybird Blanton is a good man. He'll see that his boy gets back on the right track. After our last lunch at the Pig ended with hard words, Jaybird and I have some fences to mend anyway.

"And what about Buck Eudy?" John Sparks' question startled me. He's a quiet man, and he hadn't interrupted while the youngsters told their story.

Tubby looked over at John and then at me. "Well, I expect his lawyer will be at my door early tomorrow. Am I right, Clayton?"

"Real early, Sheriff," I answered.

John looked at Red and spoke again. "Where you plan to sleep tonight?" he asked.

The boy's face showed the question had caught him off guard. I knew the sheriff wouldn't want him sleeping in the church basement again. A little voice told me I ought to offer him a bed for the night, but while I mulled over the idea, John spoke once more. "We got a daybed we can set up in the living room. It's not that big and the mattress is thin, but you're welcome to it if you don't have another place."

"I 'preciate that, Mr. Sparks," Red said. Then he grinned. "Sure beats bedding down in the cemetery with the dead people."

* * * *

True to my promise to the sheriff, George Eudy and I were waiting for him in his office this morning when he finished his ham and eggs at the Pig. I knew the rescue story would still be mine to break while I ate my barbecue at lunch. Tubby's always close mouthed about his cases.

George agreed with Tubby that his brother needed professional help and said he planned to take him to Charlotte to live with him and his wife while they got proper treatment for him. We all thought Buck would be able to recover and resume his life in

Harmony. George expressed hope that he might be able to use his training in math to get a decent job eventually.

Tubby asked a deputy to go to Buck's cell and bring him to the office. When Buck entered in his gray jail uniform, we all stood. Tubby said, "Mr. Eudy, we are dropping the murder charges. You're free to go with your brother."

Buck fixed his eyes on Tubby like he was trying to read a poison warning typed in small print and tacked on his forehead. "Well, it's about damn time," he said. When spit flew from his mouth with the words, I was reminded of his affinity for chewing tobacco. *How much will it take to tame this man?* I thought.

"Facts which are likely to clear your name completely have come to light." Tubby said. "I'm sorry it took awhile to uncover those facts."

"Another person has been charged with Eunice Gilmore's murder," I added.

Buck began to sputter angrily once more, but George put out his right arm and shook his brother's hand. "It's good to have you back, Brother," he said. For a second, Buck was uncertain of what he wanted to do, but then he nodded and returned the shake. I hope George can keep coming up with the right moves during these next few months. Maybe having a nurse for a wife will help. He'll need help, that's for sure.

After the Eudy brothers left, Tubby and I went over the case against Rev. Gilmore. First, the preacher knew for five years that Archie shot and killed Rose Byerly, but he didn't tell a soul. Maybe he spoke with God about it, but in a court of law, that doesn't count. Second, he assaulted his wife with a broom, intending to kill her, and it resulted in her death. Under questioning, it's likely he will confess to that. Number three is the tricky one. It is totally possible that he took indecent liberties with male children at his church's little day camp last summer and perhaps during previous summers. Numbers one and two are enough to put the preacher behind bars for a long, long time. If proving his manhood was what he wanted from Rose Byerly and the little boys, I wouldn't put money on his chances in any prison I've ever heard about. Even among criminals, there's a code of honor.

Number three will open a can of stinking worms here in Harmony, no doubt about it. Some of the folks out at the Tabernacle will say we should have gone with one and two and not tried to find out exactly what was in that dirty can. But we owe it to the good mamas and daddies of the little boys to find out for sure what happened out at that camp. And so we shall. Tubby said so. I wouldn't want his job for the next twelve months. Nor do I envy the lawyer Earl Gilmore finds to take his case.

Speaking of jobs, Red Byerly's likely to have him a new one soon. I mentioned to Tubby that a bit of community service might be all the punishment Red deserved for vandalizing those monuments in the cemetery. He agreed that if Red could keep his life on track, financial restitution and community service would be the best medicine for him.

For a few more moments, he looked at me without saying anything else. Then he added, "That and someone to give him a little attention now that Eunice Gilmore can't mother him anymore."

I asked if he had anybody in mind and he said, "I've often wondered why the Good Lord overlooked you and Maizie when he picked out the folks in Harmony He wanted to be parents. It's way too late for the two of you to start out with a baby now, but I wish you'd talk to Maizie about renting a room to Red. Maybe she'd fix enough supper to share with him in the evenings too."

"Knowing Maizie," I said, "she'd probably want to forget the rent part and provide it all for nothing."

"No, that wouldn't do. Red's almost a man now, and he needs to take responsibility for himself. He'd probably want it that way too. I'm pretty sure I can get him a job doing some painting and general maintenance at the Boys' Club. On the weekends he could help them with their sports program. My son Shay was in school with Red. He told me Buck Eudy used to swear Red would make a pro baseball player. He didn't have half a chance, though, with his mama dead and his daddy a drunk. He never made it through high school."

Tubby waited awhile for his words to sink in. Then he nodded his head in my direction and said, "I believe you folks could make a difference in the boy's life."

* * * *

252

So that's how I came to eat lunch with my wife today instead of breaking my rescue story at Mabel's Red Pig. If Maizie suspected anything when I phoned to tell her I'd be coming home for lunch, she gave no indication. "I have a bowl of pimento cheese in the Fridge, and I'll make us a fresh pitcher of tea," she said. "You stop by the A&P and get a loaf of bread."

We spent the first half of our meal looking out the kitchen window, where she'd lured two cardinals to eat crumbs off the porch rail. She suggested we go to a plant farm out in the county this afternoon to look for a dogwood tree for the couple to perch in all spring and summer. Knowing the project I myself wanted to suggest, I supported her dogwood idea.

When we were nearly finished with our sandwiches, I began to talk about Tubby's suggestion. His words had been convincing enough to win me, so I stuck as close to them as I could.

She sat thinking for a full minute. Then she got up, refilled our glasses with ice, and poured us each another glass of tea. She put mine beside my plate and sat back down. Her right hand came across the table and covered my left one. "You know, Clayton," she said, "we might be that boy's last chance. Let's give it a try."

That's Maizie for you.

Chapter 22

Tomorrow Is Another Day

Anybody who's had a close encounter with a murderer should be allowed to stay home from school the day after she escapes. I told my mama as much last night, but I might have known Lois Sparks would give me one of her reasonable answers.

"Jonnie," she said, "sometimes I think I bought you too many Nancy Drew mystery books over the years. You know as well as I do that if you miss one day, it's no telling how many days it'll take to make up your work. Besides, you are not sick."

"Shoot," my sister popped up. "Are you for real, Jonnie?" I knew she'd picked up that expression from Sonny, and she knew I knew. That's why she used it.

"Huh?" I said.

"There's not much chance you'll be voted Homecoming Queen next year, so you'd be smart to go on to school tomorrow." Linda Sue's statements never make good sense like Mama's do.

"Homecoming Queen has got nothing to do with anything," I said.

"Tomorrow's the best chance you're going to get to be a hot shot at Harmony High School." She threw me a hateful look. "One of these days I'll pay you back for not letting me help capture the preacher."

"Now wait just a minute, Miss Priss. You know Sonny and I only meant to snoop around a little yesterday afternoon."

My sister lowered her forehead in a frown. "Yeah, yeah," she snorted. "But still, I wasn't there, so I'll be Miss Nobody at my school tomorrow. I can't do one thing about that. You can't either. But if you stay home and miss *your* big chance, you're pure-tee stupid."

"Linda Sue, watch your mouth," Mama warned.

My sister had said enough. I went to school today. *The Telegram* will carry the story this afternoon, but this morning it was mine. Every chance that came my way, I told what the preacher said when he found us in the basement and how he chased us with a broom exactly like the one he used on his wife. I bragged about being rescued by three of the finest men in Harmony, North Carolina. The arrest of Archie Byerly came to my mind many times, but I didn't mention it. The look on Red's face and the droop of his shoulders when he talked about his mama's death yesterday kept me quiet about that story. And I didn't have the nerve to talk about the preacher and the little boys, not to a bunch of snobs who barely speak to me on most days. What I did tell caused enough of a stir.

During Mr. White's English class, three girls wrote me notes. When he caught me reaching across the aisle to pass Catherine Love my answer to hers, he asked me to bring the note to his desk, which I didn't mind doing. Heck, I was enjoying being the center of attention so much right then that I forgot how easy it would be for Mr. White to tell my daddy I'd misbehaved in his class.

Except for that one visit Miss Stewart paid us, the only time Mama and Daddy see my teachers is when the P.T.A puts on its Parents-Go-To-School Night in October. But Mr. White passes our house every time he and his wife walk the two blocks from their house on Quaye Street to his daddy's house on Gibson Street for their regular Sunday visit. If Daddy's sitting on the front porch, Mr. White usually stops to say a few words. I'd just as soon not be the subject of that conversation.

I handed him the note and stood beside his desk while he read it. When he finished, he looked up at me and said he'd like to see me in his room after school. That meant I'd miss catching the city bus and have to walk the mile home, but I nodded my head that I'd be there. On any other day, that fat hog Buddy Tarleton, who plays linebacker for the Spiders, would've snickered and punched his stupid friend Frank but not this time. Today I had the same kind of respect that comes from making the winning touchdown in a Harmony/Stanly football game.

When the final bell rang at 3:15, I went to my locker on the first floor. While I was getting my books ready to take home, Catherine stopped to ask what I'd written in the note Mr. White took away from me. I told her and I added that I wondered why he hadn't made her stay after school too. After all, we'd both written notes on the page. I don't have any close girlfriends at school and have wished something might click between Catherine and me. Right then wasn't the time to begin working on that friendship, though. I'd already upset my English teacher once today.

I hurried up the stairs and waited at the door of Mr. White's room until a kid finished asking about a question he'd missed on yesterday's poetry quiz. After he left, I went in. Mr. White pointed to a desk close to his and told me to sit down. When I saw the note lying on the side of his desk, something like a grasshopper jumped in my stomach.

"You tell a good story, Jonnie." His eyes moved from me to the note.

"Catherine wrote the first part," I said.

"Oh, I know that. I'd have known even if she hadn't signed it. Or at least, I'd have known it wasn't yours. I've watched your writing since September and I recognize your style. As I said, you tell a good story."

"Thank you." My voice was quiet and I knew my face was as red as the stripes in the little American flag hanging over his pencil sharpener. I'd been the center of attention over and over today, but this was my English teacher talking, the one Mama and Daddy had put up on a pedestal right between Franklin Roosevelt and Harry Truman.

"Next year you ought to join the staff of the school newspaper. What do you think?"

"I wanted to join this year but didn't make it. They used my try-out piece in the first issue, but they didn't have a place for me on the staff. I wish they had."

He lowered his bushy black eyebrows. Two deep wrinkles popped out between them. "Try again next year when you're a senior, and let me read your piece before you hand it to the staff. Okay?"

"Yes sir," I said. The grasshopper jumped again.

"Now, you owe me a board washing and desk straightening for passing notes during class. Get started on the boards while I go down to the teachers' lounge to check my mailbox. Do you know my gray Plymouth?" he said.

"Yes sir." *Why in the world would he ask me that?* I thought.

"Well, it's parked in the circle in front of the school. Go out there and wait for me when you finish the desks. I'll take you home."

And that's exactly what he did.

* * * *

When we stopped in front of my house, there in the driveway sat Luke's black Ford looking like it needed a good washing. What was he doing at my house when he was supposed to be working at Diamond Drug Store after school? With all the excitement of the past two days, I'd been able to keep him way back on the edge of my mind most of the time. But now, here he was. Mr. White didn't seem to notice. I thanked him for the ride and got out. He smiled and drove off.

I knew Mama and Daddy were home from work because our car sat in front of Luke's in the driveway. As I got closer to Luke's car, I saw him sitting in the front seat. I decided it was his place to speak first, so I walked up to his open window and stood there looking down at him. He ran his fingers through his hair and then smoothed it back. I hadn't put on any lipstick since lunch time, and the wind from Mr. White's open windows hadn't done a thing for my hair. Why should I care? After all, Luke Goodman had dropped me flat on Sunday night.

At first, Luke didn't say anything. Finally he looked up at me for a few seconds and then back at his steering wheel. "Jonnie," he said, "I need to talk to you."

"Okay, let's go inside and I'll get us a glass of Pepsi."

"No, I want to talk in private." He raised his eyes to my face again. "Get in and we'll drive over to the church parking lot."

I narrowed my eyes and stared down at him like he'd suggested we ought to go park in the middle of a bunch of convicts working on the chain gang. "Oh no," I said. "If I never see your

Deliverance Tabernacle again as long as I live, that will be one day too soon for me."

His mouth turned down at the corners. "Get in then and we'll talk here."

I looked down at my books. "My arms are full. I can't open the door," I said as I started toward the passenger side of his car. He got out and opened the door for me, and as soon as I slid in, he slammed it shut.

"So, what is it?" I asked when he was behind the wheel again.

He turned and his eyes shot daggers at me. "The word's out that you and Calloway and Red Byerly got Brother Gilmore in trouble."

"Wrong. He got himself in trouble."

I think Luke knew I was right, but he wasn't ready to admit it. Instead, he said, "You had no business sticking your nose where it didn't belong." He sounded like his friend JB.

"Too bad it had to be me. You people over at the Tabernacle ought to have wondered about him months, or maybe even years, ago. You yourself were out there with him at the day camp last summer. How many times did you see him lead those little boys in the Sugar Daddy dance?"

"We don't do any kind of dances at my church. Don't you know good clean fun when you see it? Brother Gilmore's a man of God and I plan to be one too."

I didn't know exactly what he meant by that last remark, but I didn't care either. I took a deep breath before I answered him. "I've seen you at Baker's Lake, Luke, and you did look mighty good in your Carolina Blue bathing trunks." I stopped long enough for him to appreciate the compliment. "But I didn't see any wings attached to your shoulders, just like I didn't see any on the preacher's back when he had those naked boys climbing on his bare chest."

He sat beside me fuming.

"We've been through all this before," I continued. "You said you never ran naked playing games with the preacher when you were a little boy at camp. I'll take your word for that. But for some reason, you didn't ask him any questions this last year when you should have spoken up."

"It wasn't my place to question Rev. Gilmore." His words sounded like a growl. "He's the leader of our church. I'm just a junior in high school."

"You're always talking about sins and demons, Luke. Did it ever occur to you that keeping quiet might be a sin? Or that Sugar Daddy dances might be the work of a demon?"

He raised his hands and lowered his head into his palms. His breath came out in short spurts. I opened my door, gathered up my books, and started for the house. When I reached the breezeway, Luke cranked his car but I didn't look back.

Linda Sue's face peeped out the kitchen window. She'd probably been there since Luke first pulled into our driveway. It wouldn't surprise me if one day soon she found her a deaf person who's willing to teach her how to read lips. Our neighbors, Mr. and Mrs. Cooley, better watch out.

The minute I got inside, she started asking her usual hundred questions. Before she could go too far, Mama said, "Jonnie, your Daddy and me talked about it on the way home from work, and we think all of us ought to go over and speak to Buck this evening before George takes him off to Charlotte. He might be there for months before he's fit to live by himself again."

She walked to the stove and turned the pork chops so that they would brown on both sides. "I did your biscuits for you today," she said. "Check to see how close they are to being done." She raised her voice and spoke to my sister, who was reading the *Teen* magazine that had come in today's mail. "Linda Sue, you need to put up that magazine and set the table. We'll eat first and then go over right after supper."

She must have seen me screw my face up into a little frown because she said, "I thought you'd want to speak to Buck, Jonnie. He's all you've talked about for the past two weeks."

"Of course, I do, Mama. It's just that *The Telegram*'s due any time now, and I can't wait to see what they did with this story."

Linda Sue chimed in. "Probably not half as much as you did with it at school today."

Mama picked up the spatula from the stove top. "*The Telegram*'s going to talk about things that happened yesterday, or a week ago, or a month ago," she said. "There's nothing more you and me can do about those stories now." She began taking the pork chops out of the frying pan and placing them on a brown paper bag to soak up the grease. "Buck's story's a different matter, though. He was a

262

sick man when he got locked up in that jail. He might be free now but he's not well. We're his neighbors. It's our place to let him know we're still his friends and to offer our help while he's trying to get back on his feet."

"Besides, *The Telegram* isn't going anyplace. It'll be here when we come back home," Linda Sue said. She loves to have the last word.

Shortly after four o'clock, the Sparks family stood on Buck's front porch. I looked out at the dusty ground under his big oak tree and remembered summer days when Linda Sue and I had played hopscotch in airplane-shaped forms we'd drawn in that yard. Buck's mama had usually brought us jelly glasses full of ice tea when we'd gotten hot and sweaty from hopping. If Miss Lillie was still alive, Buck's stay in jail would have broken her heart.

Old Willie crawled out from his cool spot under the porch. For almost two weeks now, Linda Sue and I had carried him table scraps for supper. Today, I'd wrapped up a biscuit and part of my pork chop in a piece of wax paper. He grinned and wagged his tail when he saw my little package and then gobbled up the supper I put down on the porch.

Just as he finished, the Eudy brothers opened the screen door and came out. George carried a black cardboard suitcase about the size of three men's shoeboxes lined up side by side, and Buck had a stack of books and an old brown radio. Its cord dragged on the floor.

"Y'all about ready to head for Charlotte?" Mama said. "We don't want to hold you up."

"Oh, we aren't in that big a hurry." George pointed to the porch swing and a couple straight-backed wooden chairs and said, "Sit down and let us get these things in my car. Shouldn't take but a minute."

He kept walking, but Buck stopped dead in his tracks and stood there looking from one to the other of us. "You know I've been in jail," he said. "I want to explain it to you."

"No need," Daddy said. "Sheriff Shepherd told us last night you didn't have a thing to do with killing Mrs. Gilmore. We know the preacher murdered his wife."

Mama moved a few steps closer to Buck. "We just hate you got put through this mess, Buck," she said. Her voice got shaky. "Sitting over there in the jail for almost two weeks."

George came back to the porch and told us again to have a seat. "You girls mind sitting on the steps?" he said. Of course, we didn't. It's where we used to sit after our hopscotch games.

George took the stuff out of his brother's arms, and Buck sat down on one of the chairs. He had on dungarees but they were dark blue, so I knew they were brand new. There were no tobacco stains on his plaid sport shirt. I noticed he wore socks and new loafers. I couldn't help wondering if his toenails were still long enough to curl under.

George finished loading the car and then took a seat beside Buck and patted his arm. "You remember I told you how the preacher caught Jonnie and those two boys snooping in the church basement and then went on to brag about how he'd shut up his wife?" he said. His voice was quiet like he meant Buck to hear but not us.

A sparkle came into Buck's eyes. He looked like a little boy who'd just pulled a smart trick on the neighborhood bully. "Oh yeah," he said. "Oh hell, yeah."

George gave Buck a sharp look and then cut his eyes toward Linda Sue and me sitting on the porch steps

"Excuse me, girls. Sorry, Lois," Buck mumbled. "That preacher." he said and his eyes got great big. "He'd have let me go to the pen for what he did. Maybe die in the chair. Sometimes it's hard to know who your enemies are."

"If Mrs. Gilmore could speak from her grave, I think she'd agree with you," I said.

Buck nodded. "Yeah, she was a hard woman, but she didn't deserve what he did to her."

Daddy said, "We want you to know we'll be glad to keep an eye on your house till you get back. The girls' window faces your property and there's not much they miss." He smiled down at us.

"Linda Sue and I have been feeding Willie while you were in jail," I added. "So don't worry about him while you're gone."

"I don't want to be a bother," Buck said.

"Shoot," Linda Sue answered. "We been wanting a dog as long as I can remember, and here Willie has fallen right into our laps—at least for the time being. It's no bother to us."

Buck's eyes moved around the porch until they'd rested on each one of us. "Well, I don't know how I'm going to pay you back," he said. "All four of you stood by me, and then Jonnie went out on a limb for me." He stared down at the gray porch floor. "I know people've been talking about me for over a year now, saying I'm crazy and all."

George reached over to pat his arm again. "You're better off not dwelling on that right now," he said.

"You don't owe me any payment," I said. "I still owe you for the times you've helped me with homework."

"And I know I'll wear a path from our house to yours when I start algebra next fall," Linda Sue added.

Buck gave a little laugh. "Fine." he said. "I'll do my best."

All at once, we heard horns honking. It sounded like a football pep parade was coming up Gibson Street. Next thing you know, the horns were turning into Buck's driveway. Three carloads of boys unloaded shouting, "Buck's the man! Coach, Coach, Coach!" as they piled onto his porch. Looks like I wasn't the only one who felt like they owed Buck Eudy something.

Some of those baseball players were mighty good looking. I'd like to have hung around awhile longer, but Mama got up from the swing and said it was time for us to get on home and do the supper dishes.

When we started back across the field, I felt good about Buck and about my family and about myself too. It was a little like the feeling I used to have when people saw me out on a date with Luke. No, I'll take that back. It was better.

We weren't home yet when Sonny's bicycle kicked up gravel at the top of our driveway. He threw it down way too close to Daddy's pansy bed and reached for something he'd run over in the gravel. He waved *The Telegram* back and forth over his head and shouted, "Hurry up. You won't believe the write-up we got in here."

"Uh oh," Linda Sue said. "His mama's going to have a time keeping him from quitting school and joining the Sheriff's Department."

I rolled my eyes and laughed.

About The Author

MURDER IN HARMONY is Jewel Deane Love Suddath's first novel. A native of Concord, a small textile town in North Carolina, she graduated from Concord High School and later from St. Andrews Presbyterian College in Laurinburg, North Carolina. As an adult, she nurtured two children, Beth and Rob, and taught English and creative writing at Sanderson High School in Raleigh, where David Sedaris was one of her favorite students. She has published stories and poems in small literary magazines. Currently, she lives in Raleigh with her husband George and her dog Bonnie Blue.

Printed in the United States
16533LVS00004B/55-153